Exchange is no Robbery

A Case for Crabbe and Crabbe

Geoffrey Foster

May 2012

Geoffrey Foster was born in London, England in 1933, and his childhood was mostly spent in the County of Kent, in southeast England. Some of the action of this book, which has occasional echoes of his own experiences, takes place in or around that area and in the suburbs of London.

His father was in the Metropolitan Police most of his working life, and his mother, when she worked, was a shorthand typist (a stenographer). He has two sisters, five and thirteen years younger than himself.

He went to public elementary and secondary school and then to the University of Cambridge, where he studied engineering. Moving to Australia in 1959, he taught Mechanical Engineering at the University of Queensland for 14 years, before switching to educational development, running workshops and other activities for academics. Eventually he took early retirement in 1995.

As well as writing, he likes reading, listening to music, solving cryptic crosswords, walking the family beagle, Kafka, and playing tennis with his sister Ynes.

Also by Geoffrey Foster:

Fantasies:

Kit and the Beeman	ISBN 978-0-9805310-0-8
Kit the Venturer	ISBN 978-0-9805310-1-5
Vincent the Beeman	ISBN 978-0-9805310-2-2
Beatrice's Birthday	ISBN 978-0-9805310-3-9

Beatrice and Vincent's Welsh Adventures

ISBN 978-0-9805310-4-6

Cases for Crabbe and Crabbe:

Trouble at the Mill:	ISBN 978-0-9805310-6-0
But is it Art?:	ISBN 978-0-9805310-7-7
The Problem with Janice:	ISBN 978-0-9805310-8-4
A Medical Emergency:	ISBN 978-0-9805310-9-1
An Academic Question:	ISBN 978-0-9805310-5-3

This volume:

Exchange is No Robbery: ISBN 978-0-9873131-0-2

Chapter 1

Marjorie Wentworth and Winifred Morris, the secretarial staff of the Crabbe and Crabbe detective agency, were tidying up the office on the morning after the Christmas and New Year break when the front door bell rang.

Winnie opened the door to find a young woman standing there, expensively but rather untidily dressed and looking somewhat distraught, who said, "I've come to talk to Melpomene, if she's in – I was a friend of hers at the London School of Economics."

"Please come in and sit down," said Winnie, "would you like a cup of tea? Melpomene and Alex should be here before long – we're expecting them. I'm Winnie, and this is Marjorie – we are the ones who really run the place! Could you tell me your name, please?"

"Oh yes, sorry, I'm not thinking straight. I'm Philomena Hotchkiss, but that's my married name – I was Philomena Savage at college. Have you a biscuit or something – I rushed out without having any breakfast!"

She was supplied with tea and jam tarts and settled down in a comfortable chair in the back office, but was still very fidgety and jumped when the telephone rang. Marjorie answered and said, "Oh, Mel, I'm glad you rang – are you on your way? There's a lady here waiting to see you, Philomena Hotchkiss, née Savage. Oh good, see you soon."

When Mel and Alex arrived, Winnie took them straight through to meet the visitor, who leapt to her feet and embraced Melpomene, exclaiming, "You haven't changed a bit – blonde curls, slim figure, just as you were at LSE – but maybe a little better-dressed now!" Mel laughed and said, "You look just as you did, too – but perhaps a little bit down in the dumps – you'll have to tell me what this is all about – you didn't say much in your letter. This is my husband, Alex, by the way. Should he stay and listen too, we work together on most of our cases, or do you want to keep it between us for a start?"

"Happy to meet you, Alex – at college Mel always went for the tall dark and handsome men! By all means join us as I explain – it's a complicated story."

Mel said, "Another pot of tea, please, Winnie, and more jam tarts – I hope you and Marjorie have laid in a good supply! If we want any notes taken, we'll give one of you a yell."

When they had settled themselves, Philomena started, "Call me Phil, please, I know that Mel doesn't mind shortening her name and neither do I! This bother all started no more than six weeks ago, towards the end of November. My husband, Eric, came home in a filthy temper from work one day, went straight to his study and slammed and locked the door, so I was quite worried!"

"He's normally quite placid, is he?" asked Mel.

"Well, I wouldn't say actually placid, but he's certainly not irascible as a rule – so I was really surprised at his behaviour then. I went and knocked on his study door and called out 'are you all right?' or something like that, but he just shouted 'leave me alone, can't you?' and so I went away, made a pot of tea and drank a cup or two. After an hour I went back and knocked again and asked whether I could get him anything, a cup of tea and a biscuit or a drink, and he came out then and apologized, but rather stiffly, and shut the door again, but without locking it this time. So I left him to it, hoping that he would get round to explaining when he had recovered."

"And did he?" asked Alex, "By the way, what work does he do – is it something very stressful?"

"Not for the most part, Alex. Eric works in a firm of stock-brokers in the City – not out on the trading floor of the Exchange, where the operators all run on adrenalin, but in the office. He's in charge of foreign transactions, mainly, as far as I know – he doesn't tell me much, saying that he prefers to leave his work at the office and not bring too much home with him, although he does, really – his briefcase is usually quite heavy. Anyway, when he finally emerged from his study, he apologized more sincerely, gave me a kiss and a hug, and said, 'people, people – they can get on a person's nerves sometimes!' So I relaxed and we had dinner – a bit late, but our housekeeper, Mrs Gratton, had made sure nothing was spoiled. But he didn't really explain how his colleagues, or whoever it was, had got his goat, so I didn't interrogate him further."

"You said that was how the troubles started," said Melpomene, "so what happened subsequently, and when?"

"Things went as usual for a couple of days," went on Philomena, "except that he wasn't sleeping well – tossing and turning all night – so that he looked very drawn out in the mornings. But he went off to the Tube each morning – we live in Maida Vale – and there was no repetition of that angry outburst. But the following Sunday he had a really bad night – in the small hours I woke up to find he had got up and was in his office, drinking whiskies and flicking through a pile of papers. I didn't let him see me and went back to bed. I think he came back about five o'clock, and we both got up at our normal time, around seven thirty."

"Did he say anything?" asked Mel.

"No, he just had his usual breakfast and kissed me as he left to walk to the tube station – but he was obviously turning something over and over in his mind and looking rather vacant or detached. As you might remember, Mel, I studied a certain amount of clinical psychology at LSE, and I was wondering whether it was something more than normal fatigue that was getting to Eric. I was quite apprehensive about how he might be when he got home, and this was made worse when he didn't return at his usual time. Even if he had missed his usual train he wouldn't have got home very late – the tube trains run at very close intervals during the rush hour – but this time he hadn't appeared by eight o'clock – well over two hours late! So I telephoned one of his colleagues, Frank Collins, who I know quite well – we play bridge with him and his wife from time to time."

"Was he able to help?" said Alex.

"No, not really. He had not had much to do with Eric during the day – Frank works in a different section – but he said that they had lunched together as they often did, Eric seemed a bit quiet, but didn't seem distressed. He didn't see Eric leave the office but that was nothing unusual, Frank goes home by bus – they live in Chiswick. Fortunately, just as I rang off, I heard the front door open and Eric came in! It was nearly nine by then."

"How was he?" said Mel, "Did he have anything to say?"

"He was obviously upset, so I didn't press him for an explanation – I just brought him a whisky and sat him down on a settee in the lounge. He thanked me, sipped it, and then stood up and said, 'I don't know how much more of this I can stand, Phil!'"

Chapter 2

Philomena went on, "I could see that Eric was close to tears, so I just waited. He sat down again and I took his arm – he was trembling, which is very unlike him, he's usually well in command of his emotions, almost reticent. Then he started speaking, in a very low voice, stumbling over his words."

Philomena paused, and Melpomene and Alex could see by her changing expressions that she was recollecting the scene. She sipped some tea and continued, "A lot came out, so I can't necessarily relate it in the order in which he mentioned the various points, but I'll try to sum it all up. His immediate superior – a man I've met several times in social settings, Ronald Sedgwick – seemed to be the principal actor in this drama. Eric's expression became very angry whenever he spoke about him. And as well as Sedgwick, who is the operations manager of the firm, another name came up a few times – I don't know his full name, Eric just refers to him as 'Osvaldo', he might be Spanish or something – he seems to be some sort of liaison officer with European clients."

Mel asked, "So, Phil, did you get an idea of what these people were doing that upset Eric so?"

"Yes, sorry, Mel – I'm wandering a bit, I know – the main theme seemed to be that they were trying to persuade – or even order – Eric to do things that he regarded as unethical or even illegal! I'll give you the example he told me. Earlier that day, he said, Sedgwick had called him up and asked him to come to his office. When he arrived, Sedgwick came to the door, ushered him in and then looked around the outer office as though, Eric said, he was checking whether there was anyone within earshot. Then he sat him down and proceeded to quiz him about a current transaction involving a large parcel of industrial stock. So far, nothing out of the ordinary – but then he had said something like, 'You needn't be too worried about the legal status of these people, or their ability to pay, Eric, you can take it from me that there is no truth in any rumours that might be circulating. If you have seen a piece in the financial press suggesting that Mr Hodson or his associates have undeclared interests, you may safely ignore it, I assure you.' At this point, Eric was looking particularly upset, and I could feel him

4

shaking again, so I wanted to ask him to elaborate, but then I felt it better not to interrupt his flow too much."

"So, did he go on and explain further?"

"Not really – he buried his face in his hands and started sobbing – so I put my arm round his shoulders and said 'there, there' as you do to a child. I soon found out that this was a big mistake! Eric sprang up and shouted at me 'you don't think this is serious – do you?' And then he pushed me away, quite roughly! I was frightened at this, so I started to leave the room – that was my second mistake!"

"Why, what happened?"

"He completely lost his temper, grabbed my wrist and flung me down on the settee! I was, as you might imagine, scared out of my wits, so I screamed, which seemed to break the spell. He walked over to the window and stared out, shaking his head, and said he was sorry – six or seven times."

Melpomene asked, "So, have there been other such painful occasions since?"

"Not as bad, certainly – Eric is merely morose, rather than irascible – but he is obviously still suffering. I've tried once or twice to question him about work, but he won't say much, however, to his credit he has not been nasty to me. And when we have friends round in the evening, as we did a couple of days ago, he seems to be able to forget his problems for a while and resume his former affable ways."

Alexander said, "This gives me an idea – Melpomene and you are old friends from your student days at LSE, and have recently bumped into each other, so it would be natural for you to invite us for dinner, Phil, or we could invite you and Eric to our place, so we would at least be able to see his behaviour at first hand. I wouldn't interrogate Eric, of course, and we wouldn't disclose that we are private detectives, but I could ask the sort of questions that anybody would about an acquaintance's work. What do you think, Philomena, would it be worth a try?"

"That's a very good idea, Alex, I'll suggest it to him. Maybe it would be better for us to come to your place, so that he would be away from his normal surrounding and might feel more relaxed. I'll leave it a day or two before I put it to Eric, though – I didn't get round to telling you what happened last evening, which is what prompted me to come here to your office this morning."

"Another cup?" said Mel, "This account must be a bit trying for you, Phil."

"Thanks, Mel, and I'll have another of your delicious jam tarts, too! Well, to continue, yesterday was the first day he went to work after the New Year break – the firm worked between Christmas and New Year's, but allowed what Eric refers to as a 'hangover break' to cater for those who might have celebrated to excess on New Year's Eve – Eric didn't participate, since it was mainly the young ones who celebrated that way. He was a bit late home, but not much, less than an hour, but when he did come in he was in another gloomy mood. He greeted me perfunctorily, helped himself to a large whisky and retreated to his study. I left him to it until Mrs Gratton came and said that she could serve dinner if we were ready. So I went to Eric's study, tapped on the door and went in. Imagine my surprise when I saw that he was slumped over his desk, face down, and wheezing loudly, almost snoring! I rushed to him and shook his shoulder, and he sat up and shook himself, but I could see that he was not aware of me or the surroundings. So I made him as comfortable as I could in his desk chair – he was too heavy to shift much, and went and rang Dr Grant, our local GP."

"You must have been terrified!" said Melpomene, "Was he drunk, or what?"

"No, not at all, and he hadn't even touched the whisky I'd given him! Anyway, when the doctor arrived he was let in by Cissy, our housemaid, and brought to the study. By that time, Eric was looking around him, but in a bewildered way, and Dr Grant and Cissy managed to get him to lie down on a chaise-longue in the study. The doctor checked his pulse and everything and then said that he was all right, merely exhausted, and just to let him sleep until he regained his senses and call him if he showed any signs of deterioration. So, I put a rug over him, put a cushion under his head, turned most of the lights off and sat watching him until I fell asleep myself! In the small hours he roused himself and I led him to the bedroom and put him to bed in his underwear. This morning, he woke up as if nothing had happened and insisted on having breakfast and going to work! So I let him – but I rang his workplace and spoke to the office manager, Mrs Sykes, and asked her to keep an eye on him. I gave her Dr Grant's number just in case!"

6

Chapter 3

Philomena said, "That reminds me, could I use your telephone, please? I ought to ring Mrs Sykes and make sure Eric got to work and is all right. Thanks – oh, Beryl, Philomena Hotchkiss here again – did my husband turn up safely? Not yet? What time does he usually arrive – let's see, it's 10.45 now? When he arrives, could you call me here, please, I'll tell you the number."

There was a short conversation, and then Philomena said thanks and turned back to Mel and Alex, saying anxiously, "Now I'm worried – she says he usually gets to work by ten o'clock and is very regular – what can he be doing? I hope he hasn't had a bad turn!"

"Well, there could be a number of quite harmless explanations," said Melpomene, "maybe he stopped for a cup of coffee to wake himself up after his disturbed night, for instance."

"Possibly – but they have a constant supply of coffee in his departmental office, with one of those hot-plate arrangements. But you're right, it's a bit early to start panicking! What was I going to say when this came up? Oh, I know, I was going to talk about some of his colleagues. Aside from the mysterious Osvaldo, who I never met, and Ronald Sedgwick, the one who Eric was complaining about, I have met socially one or two of his other workmates whom I didn't fancy, for one reason or another."

"Were these just your feelings?" asked Mel, "Or did they say or do anything suspicious?"

"Well, you be the judge, Mel – let's see whether your skills in social anthropology can come up with more than my psychological expertise, such as it is! I'll start with someone in Eric's own section, a woman a little bit older than us who dresses quite a lot younger, and rather flashily – perhaps my prejudices are showing, but as soon as I met her at a cocktail party put on by the firm – they do that from time to time – I decided not to trust her. When we were first introduced, by first names only, she affected a faux-cockney accent and said something like, 'Hello, ducks, come to talk to the experts, have yer?' and it was soon apparent that she had no idea who I was. When I said I was married to Eric, her tune changed markedly –

she didn't actually apologize, but she moderated her approach and started to share her views on the East Asian financial situation, which she said was going downhill fast. As I'm neither knowledgeable nor very interested in these sorts of things, I extricated myself and went to talk to Eric. Later on, I caught her chatting to another woman, and obviously talking about me, judging by the glances she was directing in my direction. Her name is Sylvia Myers – I haven't seen her since that evening."

"She certainly sounds unpleasant!" said Mel, "But do you think she might be dangerous? Has Eric mentioned her at all?"

"No, it's just a feeling I have at the back of my mind. But the other one I wanted to tell you about is certainly a threat, if I'm any judge. This is a man who is fairly high up in the firm, some sort of divisional manager I think, an ex-navy type, Commodore Lane, I don't know his first name. I wasn't introduced to him at that party, but I did eavesdrop on a conversation he was having in a corner behind the buffet with another man – as I put down my coffee cup, my attention was drawn by his raised voice. I heard him say 'Leave those gentleman to me, Peter, I'll get some of my ex-stokers to sort them out in a day or two. And don't speak to anyone else, d'ye hear?' That sounded a bit interesting, don't you think?"

Before Mel or Alex could answer, the telephone rang. Alex picked it up and immediately passed it to Philomena, saying, "It's Mrs Sykes, Phil."

Phil listened for a moment, then said, "Thanks for letting me know, Beryl – should I come there? All right, I'll go home straight away so I'm ready for him – it will only take me half an hour, but they should allow 45 minutes for safety's sake. Who will be with him? Oh, yes, I know her – thanks again."

She turned back to the others and said, "Eric passed out at his desk, so they called a doctor in the same building, who examined him and said that it was simple fatigue, just as Dr Grant had said. They will call a taxi and send him home, with his secretary, Betty Purvis, to keep an eye on him. I know Betty, she's a very steady young woman. I must say, this is all very worrying. I'm going to insist that Eric takes a few days off."

"Why don't we run you home, Philomena?" offered Mel, "It'll be quicker than the tube, and it will give us a chance to meet

Eric, if only briefly, and confirm our friendship in his view. Shall we go?"

Phil agreed gratefully, and they were soon pulling up in front of a terrace of half a dozen well-kept-up Georgian houses. Philomena led them up the steps and opened the door with her key. A maid met them, saying, "Any news of Mr Hotchkiss, Madam?"

"Yes, he is being sent home by cab, Cissy – can you make sure his bed is made up, he is apparently exhausted, and I'm going to try to persuade him to go straight to bed. These are my friends, Mr and Mrs Crabbe – they were kind enough to run me home."

"Welcome, Madam and Sir!" said the maid, "Can I get you coffee or something?"

"That would be nice!" said Mel, "We're rather awash with tea, but I'm ready for a coffee – how about you, Alex?"

Philomena took them into a sitting-room at the front of the house, saying, "We'll be able to see the taxi from there when it arrives – I'm still a bit anxious! But we're here earlier than I told Mrs Sykes, so we've got enough time to relax a bit over coffee."

While they relaxed over coffee and slices of fruitcake, Phil pointed out a portrait in oils hanging on the wall opposite to the windows, "This rather stern-looking gentleman is my great-great-grandfather, General Henry Savage, who distinguished himself in more than one exploit in the Far East, in the days of gunboat diplomacy! Our family has been much more modest since then – my father is carrying on a mercantile tradition in the West Country to this day! Oh, look, the taxi is here – excuse me!"

She rushed out and hugged her husband, while his companion, a rather stylishly-dressed young woman, was paying off the cab. Once inside, Philomena made the introductions, including Elizabeth Purvis, who smiled and said, "Betty, please – only my father calls me Elizabeth!"

Eric protested that too much fuss was being taken of him, "After all, I'm merely rather tired, not an invalid!" to which Philomena responded, "Like it or not, I'll make sure you relax and recover over the next few days – but tomorrow you can start taking me and the dog for walks in Regent's Park or somewhere – you need to take your mind off work for a while!"

Chapter 4

"Philomena and I were fellow students at LSE," said Melpomene, "so we're finding it fun to catch up! So if you feel up to it by Saturday, we'd like to have you and Phil round for dinner at our flat. Our housekeeper, Mrs Mountain, is an excellent and versatile cook, so if you have a specially favourite dish, she would be happy to prepare it. "

"Yes, meeting old friends must be good," said Eric, "I was at Aberdeen University myself, and I rarely bump into any of my fellow-students from those times, however there is one who I know to be working here in the City – but he's in an insurance office rather than a stockbroking firm. We were both Commerce students at Aberdeen – I saw him once at a seminar early last year. What did you study, Alex?"

"Oh, I did Law at University College, so I've finished up as a solicitor – rather a humdrum existence for the most part! But I certainly still keep in touch with people from my year – I suppose a lot of UCL graduates tend to stay in London and the Home Counties. Are there any from UCL who you know about at your firm – what's it called, by the way?"

"I couldn't say I know of any UCL people, Alex. The firm is called Perrin, Wesley and Associates, but neither Perrin nor Wesley are still with us – Marmaduke Perrin died two or three years ago, and Frederick Wesley fled to America under a cloud just afterwards – nobody I've spoken to will say what sort of a problem he had! There have been several debates at board level about changing the name, but a firm in this field tends to lose business if that happens, they tell me."

Philomena stood up and said, "Enough chat, Eric, dear – off to bed with you – I'll get Cissy to bring you a hot chocolate after you've had a nice hot bath!"

She took Eric's arm, he was still reluctant to leave, but staggered a little, and waved rather weakly to Mel and Alex.

Alex said, "Mel – I didn't want to mention it front of Eric and Phil, but when Phil spotted the taxi, I looked out and saw a car that I swear had been following them. I reckon the driver didn't know Eric and Philomena's address, so had been forced to keep the taxi covered – there was a fair amount of traffic around. I think it was a fairly posh car – a dark green Rover or Lanchester, or something of that class. It stayed there while the taxi was being paid off – did you notice it, Betty, or were you too busy with the cab driver?"

"I did, actually!" she replied, "I asked the driver for a receipt, so I could claim the fare back from petty cash, and while he was licking his pencil and so on, I saw that the passenger in the front seat of that car – it was an Armstrong Siddeley actually – was looking at the house and writing in a notebook or something. When the taxi drove off, they left, too. I'm afraid I didn't get the number!"

"Very interesting!" said Melpomene, "You did very well, Betty, but you couldn't be expected to get everything! I take it you didn't recognize the men in the car? You have probably noticed the clues that tell us that they didn't know this address – the fact that they had to follow the cab closely, and the note-taking, which could only have been the address, or possibly the features of the house, for a possible later attempt at a break-in!"

"Now, now, Mel!" said Alex, "Let us not go into flights of fancy just yet! But you are right about the address, which makes me think that these men were not sent by anyone at Perrin and Wesley, who would have access to employees' addresses. Of course, it could all be completely innocent. Now, Betty, I think we have reached the point when we should disclose the fact that Mel and I are private detectives, and that Philomena has engaged us to find out what has been bothering Eric at work, culminating in what looks to me very close to him having a nervous breakdown! We haven't told Eric about our real identities yet, by the way – he needs to be back in full control of himself first, before we load any more onto him!"

Betty was gratified to hear this, "To tell you the truth, I was getting very worried about him myself, and didn't know whether it would be exceeding my position to do anything about it. I haven't discussed this with anyone else at P and W, because I didn't know who might be stirring up this trouble. I have worked for stockbroking firms before, and I've seen terrible rivalries develop – there's so much money at stake that people lose their sense of morality! That's what I think, anyway! Eric may be a difficult person in some ways, but he's always treated me with respect and consideration!"

"Tell me," said Melpomene, "would you trust us to the extent that you would be willing to find out details about people in the firm, even if it meant looking into files? We wouldn't ask you to do anything particularly illegal, of course."

"No problem – actually it's a relief to find out that Philomena has been sufficiently concerned to call for help! Many a dutiful little wife would simply keep quiet and hope for the best – or else go off the rails herself in spite! In the three years I've been working at P and W, the last two as Mr Hotchkiss' secretary, there have been at least two divorces! I'm not counting the floor operators, who are the most prone to stress, but are equally immoral, and swap partners as often as they change their suits! If I had a steady boyfriend – which I don't – he would be somebody from a really boring occupation, such as an estate agent!"

"Don't be too sure!" said Mel, "Alex and I have had to deal with some very tricky estate agents at times, and in any case, it's the person who counts, not his or her occupation. If you think about your secretarial colleagues, you will probably conclude that some are dull and others are fascinating!"

"Are you going back to the office today, Betty?" asked Alex, because we'd be happy to run you there, and it will give us a chance of seeing where you work – it's quite likely that we'll be visiting Perrin, Wesley and Associates at some time in the not-too-distant future. Is it possible to park in the street close by?"

"Oh, yes – most workers in the City use the tube or the buses, and those high-level executives who drive or get driven have reserved parking near their buildings, so there are plenty of places to park on the streets. I think I will take up your invitation, Alex, as I've left some of my stuff at work, and Mrs Sykes will want to know what's going on with Eric – she's a bit of a martinet. In any case, I live further out on the north side of town, in Hampstead, so popping into work will be no inconvenience. P and W is in Threadneedle Street, not far from the Bank tube station, so I can get home by tube very easily."

They found Phil and told her that they were going and drove off. Betty, who was sitting next to Alex to direct him, suddenly grabbed his arm, saying, "Look, that's the green Armstrong Siddeley that was following us before, just parked at the end of the street – I'll get the number this time, while making sure they don't spot me – they mustn't know either of you, or your car!"

Chapter 5

"You're right, Betty!" said Alex, "They were probably assuming that you would take a taxi back to work, and they wouldn't have been paying attention to our Riley. We have adopted the practice of never parking right outside houses we visit, but a few yards up or down the street, so as to avoid being noticed."

Betty wrote the number down in Alex' faithful notebook, which he always kept in his inside coat pocket.

"I'll get onto our police contacts and have it traced," Alex said, "there's a number of questions I want to ask, too – I was intrigued when you told me, Betty, about the firm's founder, Frederick Wesley, fleeing to America under a cloud, so I'll check up on him, too. It wasn't long ago, was it?"

"No, maybe two years ago, just after Perrin died – I'd be interested, too!"

"Never fear, we'll keep you informed, now we've got someone on the inside. Here we are, this is Threadneedle Street, how far along do we go?"

"This is the Bank of England end and we're a bit further along. If you draw up behind that white delivery van, our office steps are just there, by the side of that bank building you see on the left – we're on the third and fourth floors. Thanks ever so for the lift!"

"Not at all – we should thank you!" said Mclpomene, "Before you go, tell me, have you and Eric got a direct telephone line, or do we have to ask the switchboard operator?"

"Oh, all the dealers have direct numbers, otherwise it would be unworkable, they're on the telephones all day! Pass me your book, Alex, and I'll write it down for you. Anyone else and you'll have to go through the switch. Oh, I'll give you the direct number of Frank Collins too, he and Eric are great friends."

"Yes, Philomena mentioned him, so we might find him helpful in the future," said Mel, "any others we can reach through the switch, as and when we need to talk to them. Have a nice day, what's left of it – don't forget to get your taxi fare back out of petty cash! Try and get inside without calling attention to us, in case anyone is watching, Betty!"

Back at Crabbe and Crabbe, Winnie and Marjorie wanted to know all that had happened, of course, so they all sat round chatting and having more tea, until Winnie said, "Have you two had any lunch? Marjorie and I have already eaten ours – did you want me to go and fetch you anything – I'm surprised that Mel hasn't passed out by now, knowing her appetite!"

"Good thought, Winnie!" said Melpomene, "Could you get me a cold pork pie or something like that, with some fruit? How about you, Alex?"

"I'll opt for fish and chips, please, Winnie – one piece of skate and a small serve of chips – salt but no vinegar!"

While they were waiting, Alex rang up Detective-Inspector Manley, at Mile End Road police station, "Hello, Jimmy, Alex here, how was your holiday? We seem to back in full swing at the agency, with a Stock Exchange job that could turn out to be interesting – could you look up a car registration for us, to start the New Year? It's a big Armstrong Siddeley, I'll read out the number. It followed a client of ours from his office as he was brought home sick in a taxi by his secretary. She was alert enough to spot the number when she thought the occupants were behaving a bit suspiciously. Time will tell whether these people are villains or what!"

Jimmy asked what this was all about, but Alex could only tell him that the client – or the client's husband, to be accurate – was apparently being coerced into doing things that he didn't wish to do, to the point that it was affecting his health.

"There could be all sorts of peculiar activity going on at the firm – it's called Perrin, Wesley and Associates – it might not be a bad idea to see whether your Fraud Squad friends have anything on it. Oh, yes, that reminds me, one of the founders, Mr Wesley is alleged to have skipped the country for the States a couple of years ago, which might or might not be significant. When we know a bit more, we'll fill you in more fully, Jimmy."

Jimmy said, "While you were talking, I waved the bit of paper with the car number at Cec, and he's just come back with a result. I'll put him on.

"Hello, DS Thomson here – oh, it's Alex, Jim didn't say – I rang up about that number and at first they wouldn't tell me, because it's registered to a foreign diplomatic mission, but when I said who I was they gave me the details. Turns out that it is one of a small fleet attached to the Italian Embassy and registered to a nominee called Osvaldo Scarletta. If you like, I'll see if we have anything on this person."

"Yes please do, Cec, because the name Osvaldo has come up before in our enquiries. I might also ask our contact on the international police liaison body, Sir Adrian Fitz-Hugh, if he knows anything about this man. By the way, did you say 'DS' when you introduced yourself? If this means you've made sergeant, we congratulate you on a well-deserved promotion! Here's Melpomene to add her remarks, too!"

While Mel was congratulating Cec, Alex passed the news on to Marjorie, who knew Cec and was very pleased.

"Now," he said, "Could you see whether Sir Adrian is in and available for an enquiry, please, Marjorie."

Marjorie rang on the second line, had a brief conversation, and then reported, "Sir Adrian won't be available until later today, Alex, apparently he is in an important meeting at the Board of Trade – but his p.a. will tell him as soon as he gets back."

Winnie arrived back with the lunches, saying, "I'm sorry to have to confess two failures – first, there were no pork pies left, so I got a piece of veal-and-ham pie for you, Mel, I hope that'll be all right – and Alex, the fish shop had run out of skate, so I had to get rock cod – not one of my best performances, I'm afraid!"

Mel said, "Not to worry, Winnie, it is getting a bit late in the day! I'm sure we'll both enjoy what you've brought us, won't we Alex? How about a fresh pot of tea to go with it? I didn't ask about the post – was there anything of note today?"

"Let me see," said Marjorie, "the usual couple of bills, and the even more usual batch of offers to subscribe to this or that magazine – Golf World, Readers' Digest yet again, Ladies' Home Journal, and so on. I'll leave them on the table and you can see if there's anything you fancy. And I see there's a big envelope addressed to you personally, Alex, here it is."

Alex looked to see whether there was a return address, then picked up a paper knife and slit open the envelope. Inside was something looking like one of those ransom letters popular in Hollywood crime movies, made out of letters clipped from magazines. It read 'Keep your noses out of business that don't concern you, or your families will suffer!'

15

Chapter 6

Melpomene peered closely at the note, and said, "We should try not to handle this too much – maybe there'll be fingerprints."

She picked up the note carefully by the corners, turned it over to see the back and held it up to the light, then said, "Look at this, Alex, you can see the printing on the reverse side of the pages from which the pieces were cut. Have a close look at this one, on the back of the big capital 'K' at the beginning – do you see what I can see?"

Alex squinted at it and then read it out, "There are just odd fragments of words – 'con frig', 'acqua', 'filtro' and so on."

"So," persisted Mel, "what do you deduce, Dr Watson? Do they look like English words to you?"

"Ah, I do see what you mean, Mel, I must be a bit slow today – they are Italian or something! Let's look at the others!"

After a few minutes perusing the backs of the pieces, they were both convinced, Mel saying, "These letters have been cut from an Italian magazine – most probably a woman's one, judging by the few words about cooking and household tasks I recognize!"

The telephone rang, and Marjorie said, "It's Sir Adrian – who wants to talk to him?"

Alex took the telephone, while Mel listened on the extension. After some words of greeting. Alex asked whether the name Osvaldo Scarletta rang any bells.

"Not immediately, Alex – spell it for me and I'll get my people onto it. Are you able to indicate the context at all? I don't want you to break any confidences, of course, but it might be helpful if I were to know what you think this person is up to. These days, in our work, whenever an Italian name comes up, we're inclined to think first about the Mafia or Cosa Nostra, so we have to be careful we're not getting too fixated!"

"Actually, Sir Adrian, we haven't established much of a context as yet – our client's husband has reported that he has been menaced at his stockbroking firm – Philomena thinks that people have been attempting to force him to behave dishonestly, and this Osvaldo's name was one of those mentioned. This is all very vague at this stage, I'm afraid – and, I should say that Eric Hotchkiss, the man in question, became unwell at work and had to be sent home by taxi accompanied by his secretary – then they were tailed from his office to his home by a car registered to Osvaldo Scarletta. So far, we've been kind of working at arm's length – we were engaged by Mrs Hotchkiss out of her concern for Eric, but we shall have to come clean to him and get him to agree that he wants us to be involved, so that our hands are not tied more than necessary."

"It seems likely from what you say, Alex, that this Scarletta does need to be checked out – leave it with me and I'll put my people onto it. Meanwhile, I would advise you to keep your interest in this man under your hats – we don't want to forewarn him if he really is a villain."

"Thanks very much, Adrian, for taking all this trouble!"

"Not at all, I think of you and Melpomene as valuable allies! Keep me in touch, and it also might be worth approaching Hugo Palance at the Sûreté, since the French have many more dealings with Italy than we do, and they might have Signor Scarletta flagged as a potential or actual mafioso."

After Alex had rung off, Mel said, "We ought to get this ransom note checked for fingerprints – how about a quick trip to Mile End Road nick?"

They drew up in the yard of the police station and went straight to Jimmy Manley's office, where they found him and Cec Thomson in serious conversation. "Come in and sit down, you two," said Jimmy, "we've got a new protection racket developing around the East End, but we think we've got some good leads. Be with you in a moment."

When Cec had left, accompanied by further compliments from Mel and Alex about his promotion, Mel presented Jimmy with the envelope, saying, "Here's something for your fingerprint boys – we've tried not to handle it more than we could help."

Jimmy slid the paper out of the envelope without touching it, whistled and said, "Unless the young lady who constructed this was wearing gloves she should have left her prints all over the paper and all the cut-outs, what with the pasting up and all."

"Why do you assume it was a woman, Jim?" asked Alex.

"I could be wrong, of course, but it's all lined up very neatly! When we've got the prints off the visible surfaces, we'll peel off the cut-outs and check their backs, too."

"When you do, Jimmy, see if you agree with us about their source – we reckon they've been cut from an Italian magazine, probably a woman's one, because a lot of the words on the backs of the pieces are in Italian, and they seem often to be about household appliances and cooking. You'll get a better view once they're off, of course."

Jimmy was smiling, "You know, crooks pay too much attention to the movies or the pulp detective magazines. If they did but realize it, a simple hand-written note, preferably in block capitals, provides us in the police with much less evidence than one of these paste-ups! Not only, as you have pointed out, can we find the source of the letters, but the paste used is a valuable clue, too. Did you smell this letter at all?"

"No!" said Alex, "we didn't think of that, let me try!"

Without touching the paper, he and Mel both sniffed at it, and then Mel exclaimed, "There's a faint aroma of cloves, that I remember from school-days – we used a paste that was basically made of flour and water, and they put oil of cloves in it to stop it getting mouldy!"

"Exactly!" said Jimmy, "and there are a limited number of suppliers of this, mainly for schools. So the person we are looking for is an Italian-speaking female schoolteacher!"

"You are joking, I hope, Jimmy!" said Melpomene, "You can't possibly come to such a definite conclusion on the evidence we have!"

"Of course not, Mel – I was only pulling your leg! We'll get this off to fingerprints, but I doubt whether we'll come up with an identity right away. In my view, the next task after that is to chase up the Armstrong Siddeley, and that might lead us to where its owner, Signor Scarletta, is currently hanging out."

"Yes Jimmy, and Adrian Fitz-Hugh has recommended that we ask Hugo Palance to check whether they have him tagged on any of the files at the Sûreté, so we'll try and ring him once we get back to the office."

"Why wait?" said Jimmy, "We can ring him from here! It's a while since I had a chat with Hugo, anyway."

Chapter 7

Jimmy asked the police station switchboard operator to get Hugo's number, and when it answered said, "Bonjour Mademoiselle, je veux parler avec Commissaire Principale Palance, s'il vous plaît. Ah, je comprends – peut-être plus tard. Merci beaucoup, Mademoiselle!"

"Why, Jimmy!" said Melpomene, "I had no idea you spoke French! And with an excellent accent, too! So Hugo is unavailable at the moment, I gather."

Jimmy grinned and said, "Since it seemed possible that we would be having more frequent dealings across the channel now, I've been going to classes at the local Workers' Educational Association! But what you heard was from one of the first conversations we practiced – if I tried any other topic I might not sound as good!"

"Since Hugo's not available at the moment, we might try ringing tomorrow from our agency, Jimmy," said Alex, "but what is this protection racket you were talking to Cec about? Is it anything that might concern us?"

"Not really, we think it is a bunch of strictly local hooligans, putting the hard word on small shopkeepers and cafés for the most part. One poor woman in a greengrocers was thumped a bit, but she wasn't seriously injured and has given us good descriptions of the two men involved. Nothing big enough for the mafia to be interested in. When I get the forensic information on your threatening letter I'll let you know."

Mel said, "As it's getting a bit close to knock-of time, Jimmy, could I make a couple of calls?"

"Of course, go ahead – no need to ask, really!"

Mel let the secretaries know they wouldn't be coming back to the agency, and then telephoned the flat so that Mrs Mountain could make preparations for dinner, which she found would be steak and kidney pie – very suitable for the season.

The rest of the day passed quietly and pleasantly, and they woke up for breakfast feeling ready for anything, which was fortunate, because they had hardly started on their bacon and eggs when the telephone rang. Melpomene waved Caroline away and got up and answered it herself.

"Melpomene Crabbe here," she said, and was answered by a man's voice, speaking with a foreign accent.

"Have you received our letter, Signora? I have rung now to say that you should treat our warning seriously – you are meddling in affairs that do not concern you, and we might be forced to take unpleasant actions!" With that, he rang off.

"Well that confirms our suspicions, Alex – we're dealing with Italians! It seems that they are over-confident, otherwise he wouldn't have used the word 'signora' – which gives the game away completely!"

"Unless, my dear," said Alex, "it was a deliberate attempt to put us off the scent! These villains could be from Yorkshire, or Scotland! An Italian accent is easy enough to mimic for a short while, is it not, *mia moglie cara*! And by the same token, come to think of it, it would be almost as easy to lay hands on Italian magazines!"

"You know, Alex, that letter said that our families would suffer if we didn't heed the warning – I'm going to ring Mama now and make sure she hasn't been approached."

"Good idea, Mel," said Alex, "I might check with my Mum and Dad, too, in a moment."

Lady Cynthia was brought to the telephone, so Melpomene said, "Hello, Mama, it's Mel – no, we're perfectly all right, but I'm just making sure that all of you down in Woodhampton are the same! No nasty telephone calls or anonymous letters, I hope? – Yes, yes, you don't miss much, Mama, do you – we have had one of each. We're taking them in our stride, but I thought I'd better check with you. We can't trace calls up here, because we're on automatic exchanges in London, but if you were to receive any suspicious calls, remember that they can be traced through the local exchange if you alert them first, like you did once before. Apart from all that, are you all happy? Plenty of guests in the hotel, given that it's still school holidays for a few days yet?"

The postman had not been by the time that Mel and Alex left for the office, so Mel asked Caroline to let her know if there were any letters that could be interesting. "No need to remind me, Mel, I always do that, don't I?" she said.

The post hadn't arrived at the office, either, so when it did, Mel quickly went through the letters, finding nothing but the usual bills and so on, except that there was a nice note from Philomena and Eric Hotchkiss, thanking them for their help and saying that they intended spending a few days with Philomena's sister in the country, near Braintree, and that Eric planned to try going to work again after the weekend if he felt up to it by then. In a postscript, Eric wrote that he had received a rather testy telephone call from Ronald Sedgwick, his immediate superior, complaining that Eric was 'letting the section down with all this absenteeism' and that if it continued he would have to advise the management to reconsider Eric's position. Eric added that, to his own surprise, this outburst didn't upset him, since he thought it wouldn't be any great problem to wave goodbye to Perrin, Wesley and Associates if it came to the crunch.

Over one of the interminable cups of tea, Alex suddenly said, "Now I know what's been bothering me at the back of my mind – how did these people find out we were involved, and how did they find the agency address and the telephone number of the flat?"

"Well," said Mel, "Eric knew nothing until he arrived back at his house with Betty Purvis – and neither did Betty until we told her then – mind you, she was obviously aware that something was going on, otherwise she wouldn't have suspected the people in the Armstrong Siddeley. I wonder if Philomena let something slip to anyone else at Perrin and Wesley – but I can't imagine why she would. That leaves Cissy, the housemaid – she was certainly aware that Eric was in trouble and worried – maybe Phil confided in her and it was she who spoke to someone at the firm, not knowing there might be implications. We need to talk to Philomena some more!"

"Yes, but how, Mel? She and Eric have left for the countryside – all we know is that they are at her sister's, near Braintree!"

"Let's hope that the sister is not married and is still a Miss Savage – let's try Directory Enquiries and see who of that name they have listed in the Braintree area!"

The operator at the telephone exchange was sorry, but due to staff shortages they couldn't provide telephone numbers to callers, but pointed out that large post offices kept collections of telephone directory books that they could peruse at will.

Chapter 8

"Where's the nearest decent-sized post office?" Alex asked Marjorie, "The one on the corner is only a sub-branch, I think, so it might not have a great range of telephone books."

"To be safe," replied Marjorie, "you should try the Post Office Headquarters in Old Street – there's a tube station nearby – you're bound to find the best collection there, but if you like, I'll ring up first to make sure."

"Before we try looking them up in the telephone directory," said Mel, "we should try the Hotchkiss' Maida Vale house. They might have left word with the servants about their destination – we always tell Caroline and Mrs M when we're going somewhere for a while. Can you get the number, please, Marjorie?"

A woman answered, saying "Hotchkiss residence, Eileen Gratton speakin'."

"Oh, Mrs Gratton, my name is Melpomene Crabbe, I don't think we've met, I was there when Mr Hotchkiss was brought home from work the other day. Why I'm ringing is to ask you for the telephone number or address of the place in Braintree where Mr and Mrs Hotchkiss are staying for a few days. Would you or Cissy be able to help us?"

"Cissy Partridge 'as took days orf while Sir and Madam are away, and I been give strick instructions not to speak to no-one about where they've gorn." And she hung up!

"What about Betty Purvis, Mel – we've got her direct number, so let's try her."

The telephone rang for quite a while with no answer, but just as Mel was about to give up, a breathless voice answered, "Mr Hotchkiss' office – there's nobody here, I'm afraid!"

"What about Miss Purvis?"

"Oh, she's taking time off this week, I believe."

"Thanks, anyway!"

"So, Alex, it's back to Plan A! Will you go to Old Street PO or shall I?"

"Let's both go, then if parking is difficult we can cope somehow."

Their expedition was quite successful, and within the hour they were back at the office with a list of eight 'Savage' entries from the Colchester and Chelmsford directory, covering Braintree and environs.

"All we should do is try them one by one and simply ask whether Mr and Mrs Hotchkiss are there," said Alex, "if we get into chat like 'are you Philomena's sister?' and so on, it could take a while."

"Right, off I go, Alex."

After five unsuccessful calls, Mel struck oil!

"Hello, Melpomene Crabbe here, would Mr and Mrs Hotchkiss be there? Oh good! – I'm one of Philomena's friends from college days, could I speak with her, please? Good morning, Phil, I hope you are both well and getting more relaxed. Why I'm ringing is that we have received unwelcome communications at our office and flat, and we can't puzzle out how these people got onto us – we know that you or Eric wouldn't have told anybody about us, so we wondered whether you would have any idea what could have happened. We rang your Mrs Gratton to find out where you're staying, and she, good soul, told us she couldn't pass on that information. We eventually found this number in the telephone book."

Philomena replied, "Let me think, Mel. Eric wasn't told about you until well after he was brought back from the office by Betty. She was told then, too, but she well knew that this was confidential information – she is used to being discreet at work, because information is worth money in those circles. We haven't told Mrs Gratton or Cissy who you are or even what you are doing – I might have mentioned your names at some point, but that wouldn't have meant much to either of them."

"Did you explain to your sister why you were visiting her?"

"Of course, but only in the terms that Eric has been getting overstressed at work and needed a breath of fresh air – I certainly didn't tell Yvonne that there was an investigation going on, nor were your names mentioned – there was no occasion to do that."

"So this is all very puzzling – both Alex and I are at a loss to explain it. To put you a little more in the picture, we got a warning letter to the office – made of cut-out printing pasted together, like the ransom notes you see on the Hollywood pictures and a nasty telephone call to the flat. Neither was very specific, but they're still a bit of a worry, of course, because it means they know the address of our agency and where we live. In the past we've had very unpleasant treatment from criminals, like our car being set on fire, or a bomb sent to the office – I have even been kidnapped on more than one occasion! Once they know where we live, there's no telling what they might do!"

"I suppose that now the cat's out of the bag," said Philomena, "it's going to be very hard to know what to do, except hole up somewhere secret! Would there be any point in coming here, for instance? I could ask my sister if she would be willing to have you – this is a big old farmhouse in quite a secluded area."

"That's quite a thought, Phil – I'll discuss it with Alex, and get back to you – meanwhile you could talk to Yvonne and see what she thinks about putting up more guests!"

Alex was not enthusiastic, "So this might make a nice break, but how would we pursue any enquiries? These messages are obviously intended to intimidate us – but I don't think that either of us frightens easily. I reckon we should carry on as we meant to do, while keeping a weather eye out and being careful not to take any undue risks."

"I agree Alex – so what is our next move? I think that we need to find out much more about goings-on at Ferret and Weasel, or whatever they're called. Eric seemed to be most suspicious of this Ronald Sedgwick – how can we find out more about him, without tipping our hand? And then there is the mysterious Osvaldo, of course, but it's likely that he already knows all about us – it's my bet that he's responsible for the ransom note and the nasty telephone call, and he might be working closely with Sedgwick. However, we could take advantage of the fact that neither of them have seen us – knowing our names and where we work is one thing, but recognising us face-to-face is another! I can feel another spot of role-playing coming on, how do you think I would come over as an insurance agent, or a tout for a business journal, or someone of a like nature, if I were to approach Sedgwick directly?"

Chapter 9

Melpomene remembered she had to ring Phil to let her know they had decided not to come to Braintree, and on the off-chance said to her, "Could I have a quick word with Eric, please? I promise I won't upset him! Oh, hello, Eric, I hope you are feeling more relaxed now – do you play golf or indulge in any sports?"

"Oh, yes, Melpomene – I'm going to try and get in a round or two at the local course while we're here. Phil doesn't play – I used to play with Sedgwick, at Finchley Golf Club in Mill Hill, before we fell out – he's a member there and is quite keen! Thanks for asking after me, this break will do me a world of good, I think."

Alex had been listening on the extension and as soon as Mel had rung off, said, "Guess what I'm thinking, Mrs Crabbe! Your task, if you're willing to accept it, will be to find out somehow when Ronald Sedgwick plans to play golf next! Meanwhile, I'll telephone Finchley and see whether they welcome casual visitors and how much they charge!"

Melpomene saw that she still had Philomena's last note on her blotter, so she decided to do the right thing and file it properly, saying to Marjorie, "Have you opened a file for the Hotchkiss case, yet?"

"Of course, Mel – we run a well-organized ship here! It's in the 'Clients' drawer, but there's not much in it yet, except for Philomena's original enquiry letter and a couple of our memos."

"Oh yes, let me have another look at that letter – oh I remember now, it came to Woodhampton originally, addressed to Miss Melpomene Musgrave, so she must have found out my married name and our office address subsequently. I'll have to ask her how she managed this, but not now – we've bothered them on the telephone enough for one day! Please remind me first thing in the morning, Marjorie, in case I forget!"

They were all chatting together over tea and the statutory jam tarts when the telephone rang. It was Hugo Palance, who greeted Mel with his usual enthusiasm and his usual mispronunciation of her name.

"Bonjour, ma chère Melpomène, it 'as been far too long! What can I do for you et ton brave Alex? My assistant tells me that Jimmy Manley telephoned and said you wanted to reach me, but unfortunately I was at that time engaged in arresting the maire of a small town on the Côte d'Azur and some of his échevins – you would say 'aldermen' I think – on charges of smuggling drugs and firearms! They will go for a long 'oliday to l'Île du Diable, I think!"

"Congratulations for that! What we wanted to know, Hugo, is whether you keep track of mafiosi, and if so, have you come across one called Osvaldo Scarletta? Of course, he might be an altogether upright citizen, but we have our suspicions!"

"This name rings no bells immediately, Mel, so I shall ask one of my assistants, who indeed concerns herself with the Cosa Nostra and similar organizations – the name sounds Italian or Sicilian to me, so what you suspect may very well be right! If you are at liberty to tell me, how have you crossed tracks with this individual? I assume it is in connection with a current investigation, n'est-ce pas?"

Melpomene gave Hugo a brief summary, without mentioning the Hotchkiss' names, and also told him that they had asked Sir Adrian Fitz-Hugh the same question.

"That is good – we are beginning to work quite closely with our British confrères, as well as those from the other European countries that are joining hands to cooperate. Our recent success in the South that I spoke of earlier was the outcome of a joint effort with the Italian authorities. Leave this with me, and I will see that you are informed if our Mlle Deslarges finds out anything interesting. Au revoir!"

"The wheels are turning!" said Mel, "I'm confident that if Adrian turns up anything on Osvaldo he will let us know promptly – so let's head for home, Alex. Don't you two ladies stay too long – we'll see you in the morning."

On the brief drive to the flat, Mel suddenly remembered something and said to Alex, who was driving, "Let's go back to the Old Street Post Office – I noticed they have business directories there, and we might be able to find out more about Perrin and Wesley – their entry in the ordinary telephone book is very sparse. The office should still be open, it's not five o'clock yet."

They parked in a side street and went to the enquiries counter they had used earlier, rather than lining up with the people buying stamps and handing in parcels. The clerk on duty there was a youngish man, so Melpomene practiced her demure eyelash-fluttering again.

"I'm a bit unsure of myself, so maybe you will be able to help. Do you keep the sorts of directories that would have detailed lists of the departments in large companies? I've tried a few of the main switchboard operators and they are not very helpful unless you can give them a person's name or a specific department."

"I'll show you some of the business directories we have here," said the clerk, with a smile, "and then you will be welcome to peruse those that seem to be helpful. Here is the most popular one – as you can see it's been handled a lot. You can stand and look through it here, but you might find it more comfortable to take it to that table over there."

They soon found the entry for Perrin and Wesley and were delighted to find that it listed 'key personnel' with their telephone extensions and even their room numbers. Alex copied out the details for 'Sedgwick, B.R.' and even for 'Hotchkiss, E.', confirming the number that they already knew. These were both listed under the heading 'Foreign Traders', so Alex, for good value, took the opportunity to copy the details of a 'Buchanan, I.P.' who seemed to oversee both foreign and domestic traders.

Alex took the book back to the obliging clerk, who had found another while they were busy, saying, "This is another directory that you might find helpful – it's called 'Who Owns Who', and it lists all the companies in England and their parents and subsidiaries. Would you like to scan that, too? But I should point out that we shall be closing in twenty minutes. You can always come back another day, of course!"

Mel smiled sweetly at the clerk and said, "You couldn't let us have some sheets of paper, could you? We've been putting this information in a little notebook, and it's getting rather full!"

He complied readily, and soon they were able to hand the book back, having made what looked to be very interesting notes, the chief of these being that Perrin and Wesley seemed to be a subsidiary of a conglomerate with interests in France and Italy.

Chapter 10

Melpomene and Alex got back to the flat about 5.30, and, unusually, were met at the door by Mrs Mountain, looking worried and saying, "Caroline went out to do some shoppin' about two, and I ain't seen 'er since. She were only going to the butcher's down the street, to get me an 'and of pork – it's too late to cook it for dinner now, I likes to take me time and do it thorough. But where can she 'ave got to? It's not like 'er to go orf anwhere without sayin' anyfing! I would of gone looking but I didn't know quite when you'd be back."

"Was it only the butcher's?" asked Mel, "No groceries or vegetables?"

"No, ma'am, we'd already done a big shop together this morning – but I suddenly thought that pork'd be nice for tonight! We'll 'ave to 'ave lamb chops instead, now!"

Alex said, "Let's not panic too early – first of all I'll pop down to Mr Sampson the butcher and make some enquiries. If he can't help, I'll be back and we can think what to do next."

Mr Sampson remembered that Miss Willis had come in and asked for the hand of pork, but that he'd told her that he hadn't got one left, and wouldn't a leg do instead?

"But she said she would go to see whether old Mr Potts had one, because she knew that Mrs Mountain had set her mind on a hand o' pork – she can get very particular, can Christabel, as I well know!"

"Where's Mr Potts' shop?" asked Alex, "Is it very far?"

"Not more than half a mile, down past the tube station," said Sampson, "it'd only of taken her twenty minutes without hurrying. But he'll be shut by now – you were lucky to find me still open, I'm usually shut up by about six. But, come to think of it, Potts lives over his shop, so you could knock on his door – but you'll have to knock loudly, because he's a bit hard of hearing."

Alex thanked him and decided to go back to the flat first, rather than going off on what might turn into a wild goose chase.

But as he reached the flat steps, he saw a police car at the curb, and out of it stepped Caroline, carrying her shopping basket and smiling! The policeman who was handing her out saluted Alex and said, "Here we are, Mr Crabbe, all safe and sound! Miss Willis will tell you the whole story, no doubt!" He got back in the car, which left the scene.

As they climbed the steps to the front door, Caroline was bursting to tell, but Alex persuaded her to wait for a larger audience.

After they had all had cups of tea, they sat around the lounge opposite Caroline in the chair of honour, who started by apologizing for giving everyone a fright, whereupon Melpomene said, "We're sure you didn't do it purposely, Caroline – just tell us what happened, for goodness' sake!"

She explained that after she had drawn a blank at Sampson's, she had set out for Mr Potts', but hadn't gone more than a few yards when her handbag was snatched. She held it up to her audience, to show that the strap was broken, "It was a young man who did it, and he ran off so quickly that I didn't get a very good look at him, but I did notice that he was well-dressed, in a suit, I think. I shouted 'Stop thief!' and the next thing I knew was that a policeman had grabbed him! As I found out later at the police station, where I went to make a statement, PC Fraser had been standing in a shop doorway up the street when it all happened – I think he might have been having a quiet smoke! The thief struggled and squirmed, but the PC had a firm grip on him, and blew his whistle – then another policeman ran up to help."

"So, did the police return your handbag at the station?" asked Mel.

"Yes, and they asked me to check if anything was missing, so I counted the money in my purse and checked my keys and so on. In fact there was something extra, but I didn't mention it, because I thought it might be useful as a clue and I wanted you two to see it first! If it's nothing important, we'll tell them later. Here it is!"

Caroline handed Alex a piece of note-paper, like a letter, holding it by the corner, in case of fingerprints. On it there was a brief message: 'This is another warning – don't be too curious!' Alex said, "Good thinking, Caroline, I'll put it in an envelope and we'll give it to Jimmy for testing – at least it is written and not pasted letters like the other one! But what about your handbag, Caroline – it might have fingerprints, too!"

Melpomene laughed at that, "Apart from Caroline's, the only interesting prints on the bag will be the thief's – and he's safely in custody, I assume!"

"Yes, after taking my statement, the sergeant in charge said that they were about to interrogate their prisoner, but they didn't need me to be present, so they brought me home, as you saw, Alex."

"What police-station was it, Caroline?"

"It was Islington, Alex – Sergeant Dutton gave me his number in case I needed to contact him again, here it is."

"Good, I'll give him a call, and see whether he's able to tell us any more. Most of the police round here know our agency by now!"

Alex telephoned and after a brief chat, came and reported. "I told Sergeant Dutton that we are working on a case, and that this incident might be related to it, so he said he would send us a copy of the interview transcript when it has been typed up, and one to Jimmy Manley as well. The miscreant – and this is fascinating – turns out to be an employee of an Italian importing firm, called Castelbianco SpA – apparently SpA is short for Società Per Azioni, which is like our Limited Company – which has an office listed at an address in the City. His name is Angelo Serotti, and Dutton is going to pass his details to Jimmy as well. He was evasive about the snatch, saying that he did it because he was short of cash, but neither the sergeant nor I believe him, since he was dressed expensively and had a wallet with several pounds in it on him! Perhaps he will be more cooperative after an overnight cooling-off period in the cells, or when other specific questions are put to him!"

Melpomene said, "All in all, we should congratulate Caroline, and hope she was not too upset by all this. Since it is now too late for Mrs M to cook, why don't we all go to Guiseppe's? Are you game to try someone else's cooking, Christabel?"

"Oh, yes, thanks, ma'am – I couldn't concentrate no more, anyhow. Give me a moment, and I'll put me respectable things on and comb me hair!"

So, within half an hour, they were all being seated at the trattoria, and getting ready to enjoy the meal and a glass or two.

Chapter 11

After breakfast, Alex telephoned Islington police station to see whether he and Melpomene should come there when Serotti was being interviewed.

Sergeant Dutton said, "Oh, yes please, and we would like Caroline Willis to come too, in case we need her to clarify anything about the incident. It turns out that Angelo Serotti's English is none too good, so we're bringing in DC Arturo Bellini from Shepherds Bush station to interpret – his parents run a fruit shop and they brought him up to be bilingual, so he gets called upon quite often when we have an Italian-speaking suspect or witness. Can you get here by about 10.30? By the way, this morning Serotti took advantage of the one telephone call he was allowed to speak to his bosses at Castelbianco, and they are sending a solicitor to sit with him, so we may have to be quite clever to get anything of value out of him now. As you and I suspect, this was not just a simple bag snatch! I'll try and find out whether DI Manley at Mile End Road wants to send a specialist interrogator or come himself. This seems to be blowing up into a major exercise!"

When he had rung off, Melpomene asked Alex whether he knew if Jimmy had done anything yet about getting the Fraud Squad to look at Perrin and Wesley, "If not, we could get them to check out Castelbianco as well, Alex – oh, right, I'll give Jimmy a call now, shall I?"

When Mel rang, she was told that DI Manley had already left to go to Islington, but that she could speak to DS Thomson, so she did.

"Morning, Mel – yes, I can confirm that Jimmy's oppo at the Fraud Squad promised to look into Perrin and Wesley, and also into the parent group, which is called Ward-Normandie Holdings. He hasn't got back to us yet, perhaps I'll give him a call."

"While you're at it, Cec, you could mention Castelbianco SpA to him – this is the firm that employs our bag-snatcher, Serotti. Thanks for that, we'll see you later."

Mel said, "Before we shoot off to the Islington nick, Alex, I'll let the girls at the office know what's been going on since we left yesterday afternoon – they may be wondering why we haven't turned up yet."

She picked up the telephone and was soon talking to Winnie and telling her of all the excitement, "Anything to report from you and Marjorie? Any interesting anonymous letters or telephone calls this morning?"

"I suppose you think you're joking, Mel," said Winnie, "but as a matter of fact we were visited by a mysterious woman who refused to state her business, but gave us a cock-and-bull story about doing some sort of social survey. She said she was from the University – she didn't say which one – but as she had no identification and seemed vague about it all, we sent her away without answering any of her questions. Marjorie reckons she wanted to get a look at you or Alex. So please be careful – this is all getting more and more suspicious! Will you come straight here after seeing this sneak-thief or whatever he is?"

Melpomene passed this all to Alex, who said, "I think Marjorie has hit the nail on the head! So far, none of these doubtful people have caught sight of us – they know our addresses and telephone numbers – we still don't know how they found these out – but they don't know what we actually look like. Let's try and keep it that way, Mel!"

"And I hope they haven't spotted our Riley, either – our insurance company might object if a second one of our cars happened to get torched! Should we go to Islington by tube, or is that taking caution too far?"

In the event, they drove, but parked the Riley a fair way up the street from the police station. As Alex pointed out, the opposition would already know where Serotti was being held, since they were sending a company solicitor to hold his hand during his interrogation.

Inside the station, they met Jimmy Manley and Sergeant Duncan, who introduced them to the interpreter, Detective Constable Bellini – who asked that they call him Arthur or Art, rather than Arturo.

Said Jimmy, "We already suspect that the bag-snatching was a ruse, but we should play it straight in front of Serotti and his solicitor. That gentleman hasn't arrived yet, but since we've been informed he's coming we mustn't start the questioning until he shows up, otherwise we'll be jumped on legally!"

Sergeant Duncan had a question for Mel and Alex, "Do you wish to be present in the interview room, or will you listen from the adjacent office?"

"Well," said Mel, "we're in two minds – we would prefer not to be identified by the accused or the solicitor, because we have already been harassed by telephone and letter, and we have no wish to be confronted face-to-face by someone on the side of those we are investigating. This incident, we think, is linked to a larger case that we're investigating – DI Manley knows about this and can fill you in if you like."

"On the other hand," added Alex, "it might suit us to participate directly in the interrogation, if this is allowable, rather than having to provide Arthur ahead of time with a list of points to be raised. What do you think would be best, Jimmy?"

"We would have to get agreement from Serotti, through his solicitor, for you to be present, so we should check with him first. If we had any bee-keepers' masks we could hide your identity with those – I am joking, of course!"

"You may have been joking," said Mel, "but that's not really such a bad idea – not masks, but some sort of disguise. If I were to wear glasses, and cover my hair with something like a scarf, and if Alex were to put a muffler over his mouth and chin and pull a cap down, we would both look different enough not to be recognized later!"

"How much time would you need for this?" asked Jimmy, "The solicitor could arrive any moment, and we can't really hold up the interview for too long after he's here."

"No problem!" said Mel, "Alex has a cap in the car that he used to wear when we drove the Alvis with the hood down, and he's wearing a muffler right now. I saw there was a Woolworths a couple of doors away, so I'm sure I could find something there to do the trick for me – we can get glasses for both of us there, too – they don't have to be exactly the correct prescription as long as we can see through them enough – we can always pull them down a bit if we need to read!"

So, fifteen minutes later, when a small stout person in a blue suit fussed into the station carrying a bundle of papers, all was ready. Mel and Alex were introduced to the solicitor as assistants to the complainant, Miss Willis, and were accepted.

Chapter 12

The solicitor, Mr Hepworth, asked whether he could have a few minutes alone with his client before the interview started, so he was taken to the cells. Sergeant Duncan explained to the others that he, as the arresting officer, would conduct the interview, with DC Bellini interpreting where necessary. Jimmy Manley, Melpomene and Alex could sit at the back of the interview room and observe. "You can ask questions directly if you wish, or you can speak quietly to me and I will address them to the accused – we can make it up as we go along. I'll listen to some opening statements from Miss Willis and PC Fraser first – maybe Mr Hepworth will have some questions for them – we shall see. Some solicitors get very picky!"

When everyone was assembled, Duncan said, "I want to make it clear to you all that this is not a trial, but merely a preliminary enquiry – can you explain this to Mr Serotti, please, Constable Bellini. Full notes will be kept by my shorthand writer, WPC Shannon, here."

After Caroline and PC Fraser had described the events leading up to Serotti being detained, he tried to explain, in a rapid and excitable flow of Italian, that it was all a mistake, that he had not in fact snatched the handbag, but that the lady had dropped it when the handle broke, and that he was merely intending to return it to her.

When it was pointed out that he should have said all this when the policeman seized him, Serotti claimed that he was confused at that time, did not understand what the officer had said, and thought that it would go badly for him if he objected, so had gone quietly.

At this point, the solicitor interjected that in Mr Serotti's experience in Italy, the police there were likely to be aggressive toward anyone they thought was giving trouble and that he, Hepworth, could confirm this attitude from his own experience in the country, "My company chose me for this case because they knew I am fluent in Italian and familiar with Italian procedures."

Sergeant Duncan stood up and said, "I am not satisfied with this account, and so I will remand you, Angelo Serotti, to appear at the first available session of Marylebone Magistrates'

Court. You may ask Mr Hepworth to apply on your behalf for your release on bail in an amount, in cash, which will be determined by that court and lodged at this station. Meanwhile, you will be kept in the cells here."

As Serotti was being taken away, Alex said to Sergeant Duncan, "Melpomene and I saw no point in pursuing further questions at this stage – there may be better opportunities when he appears before the bench – after all, there was no injury done to Caroline, and no loss incurred by her. This has come down to the proverbial storm in a teacup, but it might yet provide us with an opportunity to find out more about our opposition. We have already got enquiries in train with several authorities. Thanks for all this, I assume we will be informed when the unfortunate Serotti is to be brought before the magistrate."

As they all left the station, Jimmy said, "With your permission, I might drop into your flat on the way back to Mile End Road – I assume you and Caroline drove here and won't need a lift? I'm about ready for a cup or two of tea – I hope you have a good supply of jam tarts on hand, Caroline, or I can pick up something on the way, if you like – I might have some information to pass on to you about fingerprints as well as a report from CI Steve Saunders, at the Fraud Squad. See you soon!"

As it happened, Jimmy's police car was already outside the flat when they arrived, and when they went in, Jimmy presented Caroline with a box tied with string, "Kunzle cakes all round!" he announced, "I spotted the shop as I drove off. Bags I a Mint Meringue, but there are also Fondant Fancies and Macaroons for those who like them!"

Once they were sitting round enjoying their refreshments, Melpomene said, "We may not have got very far today with Signor Serotti, but maybe Jimmy's colleagues have turned up something in the fingerprint records to match his prints on the handbag – any results, Jim?"

"Nothing had come through by the time I left Mile End Road this morning, Mel, but I'll give Cec a call and find out. Excuse me a moment."

In a few minutes, he reappeared, holding some scribbled notes and giving a 'thumbs up' sign, "Success!" he said, "Our friend was apprehended three years ago as he disembarked from a cross-channel boat at Dover, with a companion who had some suspicious-looking packets in his luggage. After investigation, his mate was arrested and charged with importing a prescribed substance, namely cocaine, but there was no way of proving that Serotti was involved and so he was released. Nevertheless, his prints were kept on file! His companion, Cec told me, was later found to be linked to the 'Ndrangheta, a Mafia-style organization in Calabria, and was extradited to Naples at the request of the Italian police. So, as you can imagine, we shall now be very diligent in investigating Serotti and anyone he has contact with."

"Including, I suppose," said Alex, "his company, what was it? – Castelbianco? Did your contact at the Fraud Squad, CI Saunders , look into them as well as Perrin and Wesley?"

"Let's see," said Jimmy, opening his briefcase, "I picked up this envelope on my way out this morning. Here we are – hang on a moment – yes, Castelbianco SpA, is on their watch list, and their London office is receiving frequent visits from officers of the Squad, as well as having employee arrivals and departures logged – I see their latest entry notes that Mr A Serotti, the chief accountant, has not shown up for the last couple of days, after leaving the office without his usual document case one afternoon. Well, we know where he went!"

"What about Ferret and Weasel, or whatever they're called?" asked Mel.

"Yes, here is a note about Perrin and Wesley – I suppose that's what you mean, Mel? Steve Saunders says that his search failed to find out anything specific about them, but that there have been some problems with another subsidiary of their parent firm, Ward-Normandie Holdings, called Prescott Brothers, which is a transport firm with its main office in Birmingham and depots in several places in the south-east. The most recent incident was about a week ago, when a lorry bearing the Prescott name on both cab doors was pulled up for defective rear lights, coming out of Southampton, and a routine check by the police discovered not only that it was registered to another company but also that it was carrying a large number of cases of spirits and liqueurs with no labels on either the cases or the bottles. On the driver's manifest, headed 'Prescott Brothers', the cargo was listed as 'agricultural supplies'. As you might imagine, everything was impounded, the driver was detained, and enquiries are proceeding!"

Chapter 13

As Jimmy Manley was finishing, the telephone rang and Marjorie reported to Melpomene that a Sergeant Duncan had called, wondering if he could speak to her or Alex, "I told him your home number, and he said he would give you a few minutes more, because you had only just left his station, so he will probably ring you soon. I'll get off the line to leave it clear for him, but get back to us later, unless you're coming into the office shortly, because we have some interesting news for you!"

Over twenty minutes passed, and they were all beginning to wonder, but then the telephone rang again, so Alex picked it up.

"Hello, Mr Crabbe, Vince Duncan here, with some interesting developments to report. After the interview, I had a little chat with Arthur Bellini, saying that I wouldn't trust that solicitor, Hepworth, any further than I could throw him, and Arthur said he was of the same opinion, and why didn't he try to follow him when he left the station – Arthur had come from Shepherd's Bush by tube, so unless Hepworth had driven here, he could shadow him, no problem. So I thought I would let you know what's going on – Arthur will keep me informed if anything interesting happens! We, of course, checked the solicitor's credentials before letting him sit in, so we know that he works for a legal firm in the City – Millington, Derbyshire and Fenwick – he left us his card, so that is kosher as far as one can tell. We shall see what happens! I'll tell DI Manley as well, of course."

"No need, Vince, Jimmy's here – I'll put him in the picture unless you want a word with him now – very well then, we look forward to hearing from you later – we'll be going to the office in a little while."

When Melpomene and Alex arrived at the agency, Winnie and Marjorie were both bubbling with their news, but Mel, rather cruelly, insisted on bringing them up to date with the morning's events first. Then she said, "Now ladies, what is it that you're anxious to tell us?"

Winnie said, "Sit down first, and I'll bring the tea and jam tarts – if you can bear to wait a bit more, that is!"

"Touché!" said Alex, "we kind of asked for that!"

When they were settled, Marjorie produced a large buff envelope and took from it a bundle of papers.

"We knew you had been talking to Adrian Fitz-Hugh and Hugo Palance, and that Jimmy was getting on to the Fraud Squad, but then we remembered that Archie Staples had been very helpful before, so, instead of sitting around twiddling our thumbs, we decided to see whether he knew of any cases involving the Perrin and Wesley company, Osvaldo Scarletta or Angelo Serotti at Castelbianco SpA. Archie was very pleased to hear from us, saying that he was going through a slow patch – apparently a new KC always takes a while to become known around the big legal firms and said he would help us out cheerfully. And, true to his word, within a couple of hours, a taxi turned up with this envelope! We've had a quick look, and it seems promising, but you two will be able to judge better, of course!"

There were three sets of stapled pages in the envelope, headed 'Perrin and Wesley Associates', 'Castelbianco SpA' and 'A. Serotti', as well as a hand-written note on a half-sheet of paper from Archie, saying that it would take longer to find out about Scarletta, since he was attached to a diplomatic mission and was largely immune from normal legal proceedings.

The paragraphs on the pages about companies were mostly recognisable to Alex as copies of entries from law bulletins, and were generally of only passing interest to Mel and Alex, dealing with such matters as actions for the recovery of unpaid commissions or fees, or statutory notices of shareholders meetings and the like.

However there was one on the Perrin and Wesley list which made Melpomene sit up and read it out to the others.

"Date, place etc., etc.," she started, "now here we get to the interesting bit – 'Willingham, Arnold vs. Perrin and Wesley Associates: Action for recovery of trading losses resulting from disregard of instructions.' The interesting part to us is that a certain Mr Ronald Sedgwick was one of those called during the proceedings! This is the man who Philomena told us was harassing Eric! The claimant in the action testified that Mr Sedgwick and his staff had been given clear instructions as to the range of values within which they were requested to trade the shares of a certain company – its name is given, but it means nothing to me at the moment – but that they spent the client's funds on a large block of shares offered at a substantially higher figure. And so it goes on – it looks to me as though our Mr Sedgwick is more interested in his commission than in Mr Willingham's profits or losses. In this case, the claimant was awarded punitive damages, which would not have pleased Sedgwick at all!"

There was a buzz of conversation about this, but before Melpomene could return to perusing the documents, the telephone rang.

Winnie picked it up and passed it to Alex, "It's Sergeant Duncan again, sounding rather excited!"

"Hello Vince – it sounds as though you have some news for us!", Alex said, then, after listening, "Thanks very much for that – have you told Jimmy Manley, or shall I?"

He rang off, and related the conversation to the others, who were all impatiently waiting.

"Vince says that Arthur Bellini has just rung in. He followed the solicitor, Hepworth, wearing a raincoat over his civvies and with my motoring cap that I had left at the station pulled down over his eyes – he'll get it back to me when he can. Anyway, his quarry took the tube to Holloway Road station and made his way, Bellini following, to a row of shops with offices above them. He turned into a doorway and disappeared inside. Arthur went and had a look, finding the usual row of about five bell-pushes. One of them was labelled 'Hepworth and Finnegan, Attorneys at Law', so Arthur made a note of the address, found a telephone and asked Vince Duncan for further instructions. Vince congratulated him and said he should go back to his own nick now! The next thing that Vince did was to ring Millington, Derbyshire and Fenwick, the firm that Hepworth said he worked for, and ask to speak to Mr Hepworth. The woman who answered the telephone said, 'I'm sorry, Mr Hepworth no longer works here, since ...' and then she broke off, apparently realising she was about to give out confidential information. So he asked her to transfer him to a principal of the firm, and was connected to Mr Derbyshire. He explained that he was from the police and why he was calling, and was informed that Hepworth had been sacked for unprofessional conduct and, what's more, struck off by the Law Society!"

Chapter 14

"So, is Sergeant Duncan going to take any further action on Hepworth?" asked Melpomene.

"He didn't say," replied Alex, "Hepworth has certainly left himself liable to be charged with misrepresentation. But if it were up to me, I would keep that in reserve – we might be able to use him as a lead to finding out more about Angelo Serotti and his firm, Castelbianco. I'd better ring Vince back right away and talk to him about this. Meanwhile, Mel, why don't you see if there's anything more of interest in Archie Staples' papers?"

Melpomene continued reading the case in which Sedgwick's name had come up, and then said to Marjorie and Winnie, "As well as Sedgwick, another person at Perrin and Wesley who was accused of involvement is someone called Peter Walsh. When Eric Hotchkiss is over his recovery leave, I think we'll ask him if he's had anything to do with this person. Nothing more of interest in that case, as far as I can see, so I'll go on looking at the others that Archie has picked out."

Winnie had been looking through the telephone directory and said, "When Alex has finished his call, I'll get him to find out from the Law Society whether Finnegan, who is listed in the book as Hepworth's partner, is in fact a bona fide solicitor, or another bogus operator. At the very least, anyone who would have a struck-off solicitor as a partner must be a bit fishy!"

Alex finished his call and said, "Vince Duncan says we should go ahead with our investigation into Hepworth and Castelbianco. There's not enough evidence so far to make it worthwhile detaining Hepworth, and in any case Vince has enough on his plate to keep him more than busy. He said we could try to recruit Arthur Bellini from Shepherd's Bush station if we wished, as he seems to be a bright young detective."

Winnie told Alex her idea about Finnegan, and he said, "Good thinking, Winnie! And that reminds me of another thing. Once I've spoken to the Law Society, I'll get onto Marylebone Magistrate's Court, and see whether they have received any applications for bail for Serotti. More tea and jam tarts, please, ladies – I'm starting to feel faint, so I'm surprised that Mel hasn't collapsed yet!"

Melpomene had been going through the other papers from Archie's envelope, and said, "Nothing particularly interesting about Ferret and Weasel, but there's a reference here to do with Castelbianco that I'd like your advice on, Alex. It says, in the usual long-winded legal style, something about a claim of negligence by Castelbianco causing loss of money in a transaction that was denied by them since the employee responsible was not identified, but that this denial was subsequently refuted on the basis of *Res ipsa loquitur*. This is all too much for me, but it does call into question the honesty of this firm, surely!"

Alex smiled, "All that Latin stuff means is 'we may not know who did it, but the loss speaks for itself' – meaning that it's not important which person in particular in the firm was at fault, nevertheless Castelbianco was negligent, and it is Mr Angelo Serotti, as chief accountant, who must shoulder the blame because of his position. I'm not sure that we can investigate the whole company just yet without a lot more evidence. Anything else? What about Archie's notes on Serotti himself?"

"He's found a few instances where he was cited one way or another on his own account, other than as an employee of Castelbianco. Pretty minor stuff – parking in the wrong place plus a speeding offence causing him to lose his licence for six months, followed by two or three cases of failing to pay fares on buses and the tube – hardly a hardened habitual criminal, our Angelo!"

Before Alex had a chance to telephone Marylebone Magistrate's Court, Sergeant Duncan rang again, to say, "We've just had a call to notify us that someone from Castelbianco will be turning up to pay Signor Serotti's bail and take him away, so I wondered whether one or other of you would like to come and have a look at whoever it is they send. They said they would be here within the hour, complete with the necessary paperwork from the court. Are you interested?"

They certainly were, and Melpomene told Vince they would both come, but would try not to show themselves, "We still don't know how they identified Crabbe and Crabbe, but the longer we can delay actual sightings of Alex and me the better. What say we park up the street a little way, and then, whether they pick him up in a car or just take him away on foot, we'll be able to follow them? Perhaps one of your PCs can give us a signal when they leave – it wouldn't be good to follow the wrong car!"

"Right ho!" said Vince, "and of course we'll note the number and make of any car they send and keep as much information as possible about the people. No need to come into the station, Melpomene, just concentrate on watching for the collection party!"

So, twenty minutes later, they parked the Riley at a place where they had a good view of the police station front entrance, and settled down to watch and wait. On Melpomene's insistence, they had both brought their pistols with them – as she said, "We don't know much about these people except that they are certainly crooks!"

There was one false alarm, when a car drew up in front of the station and a man got out and went inside, but he came out alone after five minutes and drove off. A PC walked up to the Riley and told them, "He was just paying a fine! I'll remove and replace my helmet when it's the people you want."

He took up his position by the front steps of the station, and soon afterwards a white saloon car drew up. "Not a green Armstrong Siddeley, then!" said Mel, a bit disappointed.

A man wearing a coat and trilby hat got out from the passenger side and went inside. Alex said, "I expect there will be certain formalities to go through." Indeed, it was almost twenty minutes before the man reappeared with Serotti, and showed him into the back seat. The PC dutifully adjusted his helmet as he watched this. Then the white car set off up the street, with the Riley in pursuit at a discreet distance, Alex driving.

"It's anyone's guess where they're heading," said Melpomene, "the Castelbianco offices are in Leadenhall Street, so we shall be able to tell if that's where they're going before long. This looks familiar – we were here not long ago when we were taking Betty Purvis back to Perrin and Wesley in Threadneedle Street. Ah yes, we're turning into Leadenhall Street now. Let's hang back a bit and see what happens."

The trilby-wearing man and Serotti got out, and the white car started to drive off.

"I say we keep following the car," said Alex, "we already know about Castelbianco, but it might be interesting to see where the car finishes up!"

Chapter 15

The white car took a tortuous route, but Alex managed to keep it in sight, and it was soon apparent that it was heading eastward, even skirting quite closely the district where both the Crabbe and Crabbe agency and Mel and Alex' flat were located. Eventually, it pulled up in a side-street off Hackney Road, outside what looked like an engineering workshop. Alex drove past slowly, so they could see a sign on the front wall by a high roller door, through which the white car had driven. It read 'Stratton and Sons, Industrial Conveyor Belts: Tel: Hackney 5085' and under it was a bell-push labelled 'Ring for service'.

Mel was busily making notes of all this and the address – as Alex took the Riley round a corner, a few yards along the road and parked, she said, "It is very tempting to ring that bell, but we would need a good excuse for making an enquiry. Let's think – it had better be you, Alex, nobody believes that women know about anything technical! How about you say that you own a small printing business and you are thinking of installing a service lift between the ground and upper floors, and could someone come and see the set-up and perhaps give a quotation."

"So where is my printing works, Mel? They will probably know a lot of the places around here."

"Say it's in Norwich and that you will send them all the details if they are interested – you can make up something, I'm sure! You're only going in there to snoop around, after all!"

As he pressed the button, Alex could see into the building, which was not much more than a shed. Besides the white car, which he could now see was a Vauxhall, there was a large green Ford lorry backed up to a loading dock, but he couldn't make out much more in the gloom. Then a man in blue overalls emerged, wiping his hands on some cotton waste and saying, "Yus, mate, what can I do for yer? Mr Stratton, the boss, is busy – he's only this minute got back, but maybe I can help."

Alex fed him the story and the man said, "We do sometimes do hoists and such, but you'll 'ave to talk to Mr Griguolo about that – he's the chief engineer here – I'm only the workshop foreman. The telephone number is there on the sign, but leave it till later this afternoon, he's out visiting some customers. You could try to catch 'im at Castelbianco's – I don't recall the number, but it'll be in the book. I got to get back to the workshop now, before the apprentice wrecks anything else!"

Alex thanked the man and strolled back to the Riley. He related the conversation to Melpomene as they made their way back to the agency, saying, "So we now suspect that the white Vauxhall is Mr Stratton's – we can check that with the number plate – and we've encountered yet another Italian name that could be interesting, but maybe we shouldn't make too much of it at this stage. We'll try calling Mr Griguolo at Castelbianco's as soon as we get to the office and have had some tea and jam tarts, if Marjorie and Winnie haven't wolfed them all!"

Melpomene said, "I reckon I need a proper meal by now – why don't we pop into Guiseppe's on the way, Alex?"

They were welcomed as old friends at the trattoria, and offered Guiseppe's special lasagne, which satisfied even Mel's appetite, with the result that they arrived back at the agency well through the afternoon and were greeted by Marjorie with a list of telephone calls to return.

"I'd say that Jimmy Manley should be first up – he was wondering whether you'd had any success in your tracking of Serotti. And after that it sounds as though Commissaire Palance has something interesting for you, as does Adrian Fitz-Hugh! The excitement always happens when you're away from the office!"

Melpomene rang Jimmy and told him that the first call had been to drop Serotti at the Castelbianco office, which didn't tell them much.

"But then we followed that white Vauxhall and it led us to a small engineering firm called Stratton and Sons. We found out that the driver had been Mr Stratton, but whether he was *père* or *fils* we don't know. We might go back there with some spurious enquiry about installing a hoist in Alex' imaginary printing works in Norwich if it looks likely to provide us with further information. This firm is in your manor, Jimmy, in a street off Hackney Road, so we thought we'd ask if it has come to your attention at all – Alex wondered whether it might be a front for some clandestine activity – it didn't look very busy. Oh, by the way, the foreman we spoke to mentioned that the chief engineer was called Griguolo – so there seems to be quite an Italian connection."

44

Jimmy was quite pleased at this, "I'll certainly check out Stratton and Sons – you didn't get the foreman's name, I suppose? Meanwhile, we've managed to find out some other items which could be relevant. As you know, we'd already checked out Serotti, and I sent a plain-clothes PC to poke around the other firms in the Castelbianco building. I don't know whether you noticed when you were watching Serotti being dropped, but the ground floor is occupied by an Italian bank! This may or may not be significant. PC Davis went in and naively asked if he could set up a cheque account there and they told him that they dealt only with large firms in the export-import trade. It's called *Banca Popolare Di Palermo* – I think that places it in Sicily if I can rely on my memory of school geography lessons."

"Ah ha!" said Mel, "Mafia territory maybe! But we shouldn't be too quick in jumping to conclusions. Both Hugo Palance and Adrian Fitz-Hugh rang earlier, so I'll see what they have to tell us, if anything. Thanks, Jimmy, we'll keep in touch!"

Alex had been listening on the extension and said that he would try Hugo next. Winnie tried his number, to be told that he was in a meeting but would call back when he was free.

So then she tried Adrian Fitz-Hugh and Alex was put through immediately.

"It's good that you rang back now, Alex," said Adrian, "I've finally found your Osvaldo Scarletta! We have a special sub-section that concentrates on drug-running and the firearms trade, and Osvaldo was a familiar name to them. He must be a slippery customer, because neither Customs and Excise nor the police have ever been able to charge him. However his name has come up several times and he's certainly on our watch lists. Maybe he has several identities and passports, because we have no record of him entering or leaving UK over the last five years. He was interned as a foreign combatant in 1918, but was released as a result of one of the amnesties at the end of the war. So far as we know, he has been resident here since then, but has retained his Italian nationality. As I say, there have been reports which mentioned his name, but no charges. My colleague who is officer IC that section, Major Dinwoodie, says that because of your recent interest, he'll move him to a higher-level category, which means that active enquiries are possible. Keep watching this space!"

Chapter 16

"Thanks very much, Adrian," said Alex, "now we'll have a lot more to go on. Could I prevail upon you or your Major Dinwoodie to do a search on two more people of apparently Italian or Sicilian provenance who might be important to our investigation? I believe I may have already mentioned Angelo Serotti, who is soon to be charged over a comparatively minor assault on our maid, Caroline Willis, but we have only today found out about a man called Griguolo, allegedly the chief engineer of a small engineering firm in Hackney that we are suspicious about."

"Tell me the name of this firm, please, Alex, and we can see whether it has come up before in any of our enquiries. Quite often the Mafia – or British gangs for that matter – use small businesses as covers for their operations. On-course bookmakers are very popular with the criminal fraternity for a number of reasons – they cater for a very mixed clientele and they are able to disguise money transfers."

Alex told him all about the firm and its people, and, as an afterthought, also gave him the number of the Vauxhall car, "Good!" said Fitz-Hugh, "the more detail the better. Anything else at this juncture? Right – we'll let you know what comes up. We're doing a combined exercise at the moment, involving the Sûreté and the Dutch police, that concerns drug-running activities through our North Sea and Channel ports, so your information will be added to the mix."

When Alex rang off he asked, "Has Hugo called back yet? Would it be worthwhile trying again? I suppose not – Hugo is always very helpful and we don't want to harass him!"

"In any case," said Melpomene, "that is certainly enough for one day – I'm looking forward to getting home and having a warm bath before dinner, and there is a concert of works for piano and soprano being broadcast by the BBC from Wigmore Hall that I wouldn't mind listening to – do you remember our talented young friends, Olive and Gwyneth in Harpenden, Alex? – they were very keen on Dora Labette, who is one of the performers tonight. So we'll see you tomorrow, ladies!"

Over breakfast the next morning, Melpomene and Alex discussed their plans for the day.

Mel said, "My mind is working along the lines of trying to find out more about these companies – Perrin and Wesley themselves, of course, as well as Castelbianco and possibly Prescott Brothers, and even Ward-Normandie Holdings, which seems to be an umbrella organization with a predilection for dubious companies. I wonder if Jimmy's mates at the Fraud Squad have unearthed anything further about it yet – they've already mentioned Prescott's."

"So, let's go to the office," said Alex, "maybe we'll get there before the post and the usual flood of telephone calls, for once."

However, even though they beat the postman, there had already been a call from DS Thomson at Mile End Road.

Winnie said, "No need to ring back, Cec says, it was just to let you know that Serotti will come up before the Marylebone magistrates at 2.30 this afternoon – this is unexpectedly early, but apparently the court disposed of a few other cases more quickly than planned. He got the notice at the station first thing, and he expects that you two, as witnesses, will get a summons delivered by hand here, since the post might not be quick enough at such short notice. Jimmy said that he and Sergeant Duncan will see you and Caroline at Marylebone."

"Thanks, Cec," said Melpomene, "we'd better let Caroline know she will be needed."

She rang the flat and told Caroline to wear something suitable and that they would pick her up at 1.45 to go to the court.

"Now, after all that, Winnie," said Mel, "we are in need of tea and jam tarts! Ah, that's the postman at the door, I imagine."

Instead of the postman, it was a process server who had rung the bell, with a summons for Mr and Mrs Crabbe.

"Have you got one for Miss Willis there, too?" Mel asked, "We could give it to her, since we'll be seeing her soon."

"Yes, I have," said the man, "but I have to deliver it into her hands alone – thank you for the offer, but those are the rules. Sign here, please."

It was just after two o'clock when they parked the Riley up the street from the court. They started to walk toward the main entrance, when a police car screeched to a halt beside them. Jimmy Manley got out, and excitedly said, "Well the hearing's off! I'll just nick into the court and explain to them what's happening. Meanwhile, please get into my car – there's room for three on the back seat – and then I'll take you to the scene."

They piled in, and Mel asked the driver what this was all about. "DI Manley will explain it all to you, I won't steal his thunder – it's only happened a half-hour ago and our people are still getting evidence."

Jimmy ran out of the court and got into the car. They sped off, with the driver ringing the gong whenever the traffic got heavy.

Alex and Melpomene soon saw that they were heading for Leadenhall Street, and several buildings away from the Castelbianco offices were several policemen who were putting barriers around a car, a white Vauxhall, which was standing at a crazy angle, half on the pavement. Next to it was an ambulance, with two stretchers standing ready for patients, they supposed.

As they watched, the attendants carried a person from the pavement next to the Vauxhall, put him on a stretcher and completely covered him with a blanket. A doctor in a white coat was saying, "No hurry to get this one back to the hospital, he'll keep until we've had a look at his companion – if we can get him out, that is."

Alex and Melpomene could see what he meant – the white car was stove in, so the passenger was trapped in his seat. Two of the policemen managed to wrench open the door, and the doctor leant in and put his hand on his throat.

"No pulse here, either. But try not to damage him further as you get him out – I still have to do an autopsy, even though I can tell right now that the cause of death in both cases was probably something to do with the bullet holes in their heads!"

Caroline was looking rather green, so Melpomene hugged her and murmured comforting words to her.

Jimmy said, "I'd better fill in the details for you, although you can maybe guess a lot of them. So far, we have one eye-witness, who has been taken to the station so she can be questioned properly, but she could tell us that when the car started to drive off, a large man – in city clothes, she said – ran across the road and shot out the side window first and then the occupants. The car then veered across the road and hit a lamp-post. Someone in a shop rang for police and an ambulance. The assailant made his escape while most of the bystanders were just gawping."

Chapter 17

Jimmy Manley asked the doctor where the casualties would be taken for autopsy.

"I shall travel back with the ambulance to University College Hospital, as I'm on duty in accident and emergency there today – I've drawn the short straw and will be doing the p.m. as well. As I said before, it seems that it'll be quite straightforward to establish the proximate cause of death, but I will go through the whole procedure for the benefit of the students attending. I'll send copies of the reports to you, Detective-Inspector Manley – at which police station, please? My name is Calvert Norton, if you need to contact me."

"If you don't mind, Dr Norton," said Jimmy, "I'll collect the contents of their pockets now – and if you'll forgive me for mentioning it, I imagine that you would take note of any distinguishing features, such as previous injuries or scars, or tattoos, and include these in the report for us."

"Of course, of course! I gather from your presence here, Detective-Inspector, and from the bullet wounds, that these men are not simple accident victims! I should be able to present my reports to you before noon tomorrow – if I strike any difficulty with making this deadline I will telephone you."

Jimmy searched the pockets of the two bodies inside the ambulance with the doors shut, as there was still quite a throng of fascinated bystanders. After a few minutes he reappeared, thanked the doctor, and the ambulance drove off.

Two of the policemen had taken the opportunity of asking around the crowd whether anyone else had seen the gunman, apart from the woman who had been taken to the station earlier, and they informed Jimmy that there were two more people who were prepared to make statements. One was an elderly paper-seller whose stand was close to where the white car had finished up, and the other was a boy scout, about thirteen, who was jumping up and down, eager to tell his story.

The paper seller was reluctant to leave his stack of papers, so Jimmy asked a PC to take his statement, "And get his name and address, in case we need to see him again", while the boy scout, who said his name was Les White, would be taken to Mile End

Road. Until Caroline, Mel and Alex were dropped back at Marylebone where they had parked the Riley, he had to squeeze in the back of Jimmy's car with them, but nevertheless he was thrilled to be in a police car, saying, "Are you being arrested, or are you witnesses like me?"

Melpomene explained to him that Miss Willis was a witness in another case, but that she and Alex were private detectives. "Like Sexton Blake or Hercule Poirot?" he asked, with his eyes shining, and then promised he would keep their identities secret.

As they were dropped at their car, Jimmy said, "Give me a call in an hour or so, and I'll tell you what we've found out about the two victims and, if anything, about the murderer."

Caroline asked if she could be taken to the office, as she was interested in what Jimmy would find out, and she also wanted to have a chat with Winnie and Marjorie, as she didn't get a chance to socialize with them very often.

"I'm getting famished," said Melpomene, "it's ages since lunch now! So we'd better collect something on the way to eat in the office, in case the secretaries have wolfed everything!"

In the event, they had no difficulty in making a meal with the selection of French loaves and pâté they bought at a superior grocers in the city.

Of course, Melpomene had to relate the earlier excitement to the secretaries, which was especially appreciated by Winnie, who liked a bit of violence from time to time, so long as she was not involved – as she said!

And as they were all contemplating finishing for the day, the telephone rang, and it was Jimmy, who had just heard from Dr Norton.

"He told me that there were no signs of alcohol or drugs, but that the passenger, Serotti, would have been killed by the crash anyway, without needing the bullet, as his neck was broken – he also had signs that his thigh had been broken and healed some years ago. Calvert Norton retrieved the bullet from the driver's brain, but Serotti had an exit wound, so his bullet will probably be lodged in the car somewhere. The forensics people will look out for it, while they are gathering fingerprints and evidence from that Vauxhall car. As you know, I went through their pockets, and found a letter that Serotti had received while he was in the nick. We shall check that out thoroughly, given time, but it looked like a personal letter, which is why the people looking after the cells had allowed him to keep it. The driver had a driving licence in the name of 'Walter Mason', but it looked suspicious to me – the forensics officers have tests for such things – so it might not tell us much. The driver was wearing a very nice rolled-gold Swiss wrist-watch, which looked as though it cost a bob or two, and his suit and shirt were tailored and of very good quality, too, in contrast to Serotti, who looked as though he had been outfitted from top to toe by Marks and Spencer – clothes of reasonably good quality but certainly not at the top of the market. Their shoes showed a similar contrast in style and quality. The driver had a five-pointed star tattooed on his right hand between the thumb and index finger – it's possible this is some sort of Mafia identification – I'll ask Adrian Fitz-Hugh if his Italian contacts know about this. Apart from what I've mentioned, and their fingerprints, if they are on our files, there were no other clues to the identity of either of these gentlemen."

"That sounds pretty comprehensive!" said Alex, "I suppose you will be able to identify the gun that was used by examining the bullet."

"That's right, Alex, Calvert Norton is sending his written report and the bullet to us later – he told me the other things over the telephone. I'm waiting for Cec Thomson's notes that he and a PC have been taking from the witnesses – a Mrs Susan Butterworth, who saw the whole thing, and young Les White, the boy scout, who said he had a good look at the gunman. That paper-seller was not very helpful – he was very excited, because the car came right up onto the pavement where he was standing, and he was hardly coherent at the time – I'm not betting on getting very much from him later, either."

"Thanks for all that, Jimmy!" said Alex, "I'm particularly interested to find whether Adrian Fitz-Hugh comes up with any Mafia connections – we've been wondering if they are involved, given the Italian angles we've been noticing."

"Right, Alex, when I know more I might visit you in your office. By the way, what's happening with your original client, Eric Hotchkiss – is he still in Essex? He will have a lot of catching-up to do, and might be able to fill in some of our gaps. I'll see you all later! Sleep well and don't dream about murders!"

Chapter 18

Melpomene and Alex – and Caroline, too – had a very quiet evening, welcome after such a hectic day. Alex caught up with the newspapers and Melpomene with the Times cryptic crosswords that she had missed, and then they were ready for bed, earlier than usual.

The next morning they enjoyed a substantial breakfast – as Mel remarked, "We ought to stoke up well, in case we have another day full of alarums and excursions!"

They arrived at the agency good and early, and were met at the door by Winnie, saying, "There's a list of telephone calls for you to answer – from Hugo Palance, Sir Adrian, Jimmy Manley of course, and even Eric Hotchkiss, calling from his office at Perrin and Wesley! Which one do you want to deal with first?"

"I'll take Hugo, I think, Winnie," said Melpomene, "but do you want to call Adrian Fitz-Hugh at the same time, Alex?"

"No, I think I'll talk to Jimmy first, Mel, he might have some information about yesterday's driver that would be worth passing to Adrian."

Commissaire Principale Palance was profuse with apologies when Melpomene spoke to him. "I really intended to telephone you yesterday, Melpomène, but as you English say, I was all over the place like the breakfast of a madwoman! We have had a bourrasque of kidnappings in the coastal towns of Boulogne and St Malo, so we are stretched to the limit – not much success with them, yet! But, what I wanted to tell you was that my assistant, Hortense Deslarges, has indeed come across the name Osvaldo Scarletta, in connection with currency transfers through a bank in Lyons that we have been suspicious of for some time. We have chosen not to intervene, but have been watching it closely – we even managed to have one of our agents employed in the mailroom there. It seems likely that several accounts at that bank, registered in the names of what appear to be legitimate businesses, receive funds from overseas countries including England, and forward them on to firms in Bologna, Milan and Naples who have known mafia connections. I should say, however, that I have gained the impression that very few companies in Italy are completely clear of such connections, often even at board level. Now we have identified Signor Scarletta, we will keep our eyes on him. Mlle Deslarges thinks he is in London at the moment. Is all this of any help to you, ma chère? If you wish to speak to Hortense, I will give you her direct number. Her English is much better than mine, and she is also fluent in Italian, Sicilian and Milanese, as well as being a qualified accountant!"

Mel thanked Hugo and rang off and asked Alex what Jimmy had to tell him.

"Fortunately, he found that the driver's prints were on file – it turns out that his name is Ernie Hopkins – I was kind of hoping he would be another Italian! He is – was – a fairly small-time villain, with one jail term of two years for vehicle theft with violence – he pulled a woman who had stopped to give him a lift out of her car and drove off with it! She wasn't seriously injured – barked knees and bruising to the body – but that was counted as grievous bodily harm by the magistrate. He had a few fines too, for a variety of traffic offences, mostly speeding."

"Was there anything interesting arising from the autopsies?" asked Mel.

"Not much – as Dr Norton guessed at the scene, Serotti's neck was broken and that would have caused his death anyway, without being shot. There was some alcohol in the driver's bloodstream, but probably not enough to affect his driving. By the way, the bullets retrieved from the car and the one found during autopsy were of a calibre that is used by several types of gun, including your Beretta, Mel, a pistol popular with Mafiosi – nice to be in good company!"

"Good to know, Alex! Any more?"

"Then Jimmy told me about the information they got from the witnesses, Mrs Susan Butterworth, and young Les White – in short, not very much. Both report that the assassin was male, tall and dressed in business clothes. Mrs Butterworth thought he might have had an overcoat on, but Les didn't think so. The lady lost sight of him once the shooting was done and the car mounted the pavement, but our observant boy scout says that he watched him cross back over the road and hurry away, but walking fast rather than running. He went in the direction of the crossroads and Les lost sight of him then, but he says that he had rather long black hair, no hat. Jimmy said that he didn't expect very much more, Mel, eyewitnesses are not very informative, in his experience. What I'm going to do next, Mel, is ring Adrian Fitz-Hugh – but I need tea and jam tarts first – did you get that, Winnie or Marjorie?"

Mel said, "Hear hear! And I am going to try to call Eric at Perrin and Wesley – I'm somewhat surprised he is back at his desk so soon. How did he sound when he rang, Winnie?"

"Pretty normal, Mel, he didn't give me the impression he was worried or upset."

"Right, have you got his direct number there? Here we go – Oh, Eric, Melpomene here, good to speak to you! Are you back in the swing yet? – We've got some news for you, too! You go first."

Eric said, "Everything seems normal here, Melpomene. As soon as I arrived, I had a chat with my secretary, Betty Purvis – you've met her, of course – and she told me that there had been no problems because of my absence. She had managed to convince management, including Ronald Sedgwick, that I was merely over-tired and had been advised to take a short break, and would be back on deck as soon as I was recovered. In our business, which can be rather intense and stressful, reactions like this, even complete nervous breakdowns, are not unknown. I have an appointment with Sedgwick later this morning, but, strangely, I feel quite calm about this – I think he just wants to know what my immediate programme is going to be."

"That sounds quite encouraging, Eric! Tell me, have you had dealings with a firm called Castelbianco? And particularly, with one of their employees, Angelo Serotti? I'll tell you why I ask in a moment."

"Yes, Mel, Castelbianco is a firm whose shares I have traded in from time to time, but I have never had any contact with anyone working there, and the name Serotti rings no bells for me. What's this all about?"

Mel then related the whole story to him, starting with the snatched bag and finishing with the murders, "But we have no idea whether your company, or you personally, are in some way the targets of this bizarre episode. But what it has prompted, Eric, is a whole investigation into what might be illegal money transfers, possibly involving the Sicilian mafia. We are working with police forces in several countries on this. There is no need to take action at this stage, Eric, but, as an insider, you could be a valuable informant in the future!"

54

Chapter 19

Eric said, "You know, Melpomene, while I was away in Braintree I had plenty of time to think about the job – I even seriously contemplated leaving P and W altogether – but in the end I thought that after all it is a reasonably well-paid occupation that I'm fairly good at and that I ought to find ways of not letting the back-biting get to me – in any company there will always be petty jealousies and rivalries. Having come to that conclusion, I'm now sure that I would be willing to help you and Alex to try to get to the bottom of whatever skullduggery there is that's going on behind the scenes – there must be something, and your idea about illegal money transfers is certainly one possibility to consider."

"I'm very glad to hear you say that, Eric! Once you've settled back in a bit and found out what Mr Sedgwick intends for you, we must all put our heads together – and Betty Purvis, too, if you think that would be a good idea. But you know, Eric, Alex and I are still puzzled about a few things. How was it that the people who sent us those anonymous letters and made the threatening telephone calls knew that the Crabbe and Crabbe agency was involved? And what has Angelo Serotti – I should say the late Angelo Serotti – to do with any of this? And, lastly, how does the mysterious Signor Osvaldo Scarletta play a part?"

"Thanks, Melpomene," said Eric, "after I've seen Ronald Sedgwick, and talked to some other people here, including my friend Frank Collins, as well as Mr Buchanan, who has overview of all the dealings, domestic and foreign, I'll ring you again and let you know what's happening."

The conversation about the anonymous letters and threatening calls had set Melpomene thinking. She thought she might discuss it with Alex, but saw he was still talking on the telephone, so she went and felt the teapot to see whether it was still warm enough for another cup. It wasn't, so she filled up the kettle and put it on the gas. Then Alex came into the kitchen on a similar mission.

"Were you talking to Adrian?" Mel asked him.

"I certainly was, and he had some very interesting news for us – let's grab our teas and jam tarts and I'll tell you all about it."

They sat down and Alex said, "It's good that we're establishing a functioning network, Mel – Adrian started by telling me that Jimmy had given him as many details as he had about the driver of the white Vauxhall, the so-called Ernie Hopkins. Adrian passed the name to one of his staff, and while they were waiting to see whether anything was known about him, he told Jimmy that his people had struck oil with both Angelo Serotti and the shadowy Osvaldo Scarletta. One of Adrian's associates, Mario Donizzetti, has worked with Hortense Deslarges of the Sûreté previously. He had already amassed quite an extensive file on Signor Scarletta, so these two were able to share their information and, between them, fill in the gaps. In particular, they came up with a list of people associated with Scarletta, in England and overseas, mainly Sicily, indicating that he seems to be an important link between the Mafia and a widespread organization with lairs in various places in the East End, that are active in the illicit cross-channel trade in guns and narcotics. And Angelo Serotti appears to be Scarletta's contact or agent, covering a number of firms, including, of course, Perrin and Wesley and Castelbianco. I thanked him very much, and he invited us, in a few days, to another of the regular meetings that are being held in rotation among the countries whose police forces are collaborating, on this occasion in London."

"What a pity!" said Melpomene, "It would be nice to visit Amsterdam or Copenhagen or Paris once in a while – maybe we'll have a chance later! Apart from that, Alex, I've still been fretting about what let the cat out of the bag concerning Crabbe and Crabbe's involvement with l'affaire Hotchkiss – what I might do is go back to something we know for certain, namely that Philomena tried at first to reach me at Woodhampton, under my maiden name of Musgrave, and then try to trace the subsequent events. It's about time I had a conversation with Mama, in any case – I wonder that she hasn't been ringing up daily to check that we're safe."

Lady Cynthia was indeed, very pleased to hear from Melpomene, but said, "Now I'm not going to fuss – I've convinced myself that you and Alex are adults and can look after yourselves! I have to admit that I was on the point of telephoning you when I read about that dreadful shooting in the City, but I told myself that there was little chance you would be involved!"

"Actually, Mama dearest, we *were* involved – but thankfully not present at the actual murder scene this time! I'll tell you all about it later, it's related to the job we are doing for Philomena Hitchcock and her husband, and as it happens, I telephoned to ask you about this very case. You will recall that Philomena is an old friend from LSE – she wrote to me care of the castle as Melpomene Musgrave. You, as you say, brought her up to date, and we subsequently got a letter from her at Crabbe and Crabbe, which we proceeded to follow up, of course. What has been puzzling us is that other people, possibly criminals, have discovered our agency address and that of our flat, when Philomena hadn't even mentioned these to her husband Eric, let alone anyone else! He was having difficulties at his work, so she was being very cautious, not knowing quite who was responsible. Can you recall how it was that Philomena was told where we were? Did you telephone her, or what? I know you are always very reticent in matters relating to our work, dear Mama, so I'm certainly not accusing you of careless talk!"

"I can recall the events quite clearly, Mel. Yes, I did telephone her – she had put her number on her letter. I'm sure I told her nothing more than your married name and the addresses and telephone numbers of the agency and your flat. But I will check the file – I'm in my office now, excuse me a second while I go to the filing cabinet – ah, here we are. In your file, there's her original letter and my hand-written memo, noting that I had told her those things, but there's also a copy of a letter that I haven't seen before, which must have been written by my new secretary, Mavis Barnard, who is very business-like and keen – she used to work for a firm of solicitors in Woodhampton. Let me see – it's simply a confirmation of my telephone message to Philomena, but she's sent it to Mr Phillip Hotchkiss c/o Messrs Perrin and Wesley. She must have looked up the address, because only the firm's name was given in the original enquiry. Very puzzling!"

"Oh, Mama, I think I know what's happened – please look at Philomena's original letter – I bet she's signed it 'Phil' – she hardly ever uses her full name, just as I usually call myself 'Mel'! – How would Mavis know that the writer was a woman! I'll bet her reply was passed around from desk to desk at P&W – I don't think it ever got to Eric, otherwise he would have confronted Philomena with it – he was very upset at the time!"

"I'll have a quiet word with Mavis!" said Lady Cynthia.

Chapter 20

After chatting about more trivial topics a bit longer with her Mama, Melpomene hung up and turned to Alex, saying, "That's one worry off my chest, at least!" and told him the story.

He replied, "So here we are, sitting here in possession of quite a body of information! What we need to do next is devise some ways of following it up. We should try and engage somehow with one or more of these villains – while, of course, taking care they don't take advantage of this – we've already been warned off in no uncertain terms! By the way, did we ever get any results from the fingerprints on the anonymous letter? And another thing, I should try telephoning Hugo's assistant, Hortense Deslarges, first of all simply to make contact, but also to ask her about Osvaldo."

"Right, Alex," said Melpomene, "while you're doing that I'll call Jimmy about the fingerprints – he should be back at Mile End Road by now."

When Mlle Deslarges was brought to the telephone, she was quite keen to talk. Alex was interested to hear that her English was almost free of any French accent and complimented her on this, "Mai oui, monsieur, I am very glad to 'ear you say zis!" she said, in an exaggerated stage French accent, and then dropped back to English, "I pursued part of my education in the Faculty of Modern and Medieval Languages at Cambridge. I am told that my standard Italian and my Italian dialects are equally impressive – I have, I suppose, a natural facility in this respect – what is known as a 'good ear'. Now, Alex, if I may address you thus, I'm sure you did not telephone me to discuss my accent!"

"I believe you have some information on a certain Osvaldo Scarletta – we have suspicions that he might be a Mafioso – what do you know about him – and, while I think of it, would a tattoo of a five-pointed star have any significance? We have a shooting victim with such a star between his thumb and forefinger."

"Your suspicions are accurate, Alex – we have evidence that Signor Scarletta has been involved in mafia-style activities in several regions of Italy and Sicily. On one recent occasion, the

Carabinieri in San Remo seized five men in a speedboat in the harbour with a cargo of handguns and machine guns, about to leave for either France or Morocco. Scarletta was spotted on the quayside and taken in for questioning, but was able to evade arrest, one way or another – probably, in my opinion, by bribery! As for the star tattoo, this is a membership emblem used by several Calabrian and Sicilian 'families'. Who did you see with such a tattoo – you say it was a shooting victim – who shot him, Alex? I hear from Commissaire Palance that your partner Melpomene is good with a pistol!"

"Not this time, Hortense!" and Alex related the incident outside the Castelbianco building, then going on, "The shot driver was the one with the star – his fingerprints were on file under the name of Ernie Hopkins, but I have my doubts about the truth of that, given his Italian connections. The shooter is still at large, I regret to say – the eye-witnesses were not very helpful, one saying he had long black hair, but that was about all we could find out, other than he was tall. Have you any up-to-date information on Scarletta's usual location? The police here have been keeping a lookout for an Armstrong Siddely car that is registered to him as a nominee of the Italian Embassy, but there have been no sightings yet. That was the same car that followed our client from his work address to his home, but that's all we know about it."

"I can help a little with Scarletta's movements," said Hortense, "after the incident at San Remo when the authorities could find nothing to hold him on, an agent of the Sûreté was detailed to track him, so I can tell you that he proceeded immediately to Le Havre, crossed La Manche and went directly by public transport to the Italian Embassy, near Grosvenor Square. Our agent kept watch outside, but he might have left by another exit. This was only yesterday, so it is likely that he is still in that district. We know that the embassy has leases on several houses and apartments nearby. If you wish, I will supply this information for enabling a discreet house-to-house search, preferably by members of the Metropolitan Police – we have established cordial relations with your Detective-Inspector Manley. By the way, Scarletta is tall and has long black hair – not that this proves anything!"

"Thank you so much, Hortense!" said Alex, "I predict that our collaboration will become increasingly fruitful in the future!

Please give my regards to Hugo Palance when you see him next."

While Alex had been talking to Mlle Deslarges, Mel had been asking Jimmy whether there had been any results from the fingerprint testing of the pasted-up anonymous letter and interior of the Vauxhall car.

"Taking the car first," he replied, "we found plenty of Serotti's prints and those of the driver, whatever his real name will turn out to be, but there were prints from at least five others, some of whom will be found to be mechanics and so on, I suppose. The fingerprint boys are carrying on looking for matches in our files as we speak. Even if these people have police records, this doesn't necessarily mean that they are important for our current investigation."

"Well, we won't hold our breath!" said Mel, "What about that letter?"

"This is very interesting, we think – as I surmised earlier, the pasting up was indeed done by a woman. You may remember that I kidded you at the time that we were looking for an Italian-speaking female schoolteacher! That was a joke then, but it turns out that it was not all that wide of the mark! The prints on file are those of a woman called Cinzia Preston, née Tagliamonte, who was charged with a minor spot of shop-lifting in Harrods some three or four years ago. Since then, she has mended her ways and is at present employed by the Italian Embassy as an English tutor to some of the diplomats' young children."

"Do we know anything about Mr Preston?" asked Melpomene.

"Only that he and Cinzia live in a mews flat not very far from the embassy – we haven't found yet where Preston works or what he does for a living. So we've got the beat policemen casting an occasional eye over the place – not constant surveillance, we can't afford the time or staff for that. I have another fingerprint result, by the way. Do you remember that I found a letter in Serotti's inside pocket when I searched his body?"

"Yes, Jimmy, you said he'd been allowed to keep it in the station lock-up because it looked like a personal letter. So you got some significant prints off that too, did you?"

"We certainly did, but you won't guess whose straight away!"

Chapter 21

"Come on, Jimmy," said Melpomene, "don't be a tease – I'm not going to get into guessing games with you – who was it?"

"You'll remember that the late Angelo Serotti was detained at Dover a few years back, in company with someone carrying cocaine in his luggage. We had to let Serotti go then, but the other was arrested and subsequently extradited to Italy, on the request of the Naples police. His name was Gian Carlo Passarella, and he was well-known by them as a member of the Camorra. Like many another Mafioso, he spent very little time in custody, and is now thought to be in England, we haven't found where. Anyway, they were his fingerprints on Serotti's letter, so our experts had another look at it. We now think it was a coded message, not a personal letter! Have you ever played games of acrostics, Mel? Let me read that letter to you – start every new line when I say so. Got a pencil and paper? Here we go!"

Melpomene listened carefully, and when Jimmy had finished dictating, she had the following lines written out:

> *Mother heard you were poorly, hope you shake it off*
> *Even if you feel bad, it won't last for ever*
> *Eat well – stick to spaghetti!*
> *Try to get plenty of rest in bed*
> *Unless I see you soon, say hello to Lisa*
> *Some time we'll all have a holiday*
> *Up to you when we can*
> *All the best, behave!*
> *Love, XXX.*

Jimmy said, "So what does the acrostic read now, Mel?"

"Not hard, Jimmy – 'meet usual Friday nex'. Well, we know that Serotti's not going to meet anyone on the next or any other Friday! What a pity! But at least this tells us that Signor Passarella is involved, which in turn is an indication that there is something illegal – gun running or drugs – going on here. We can also surmise that a person or persons at Stratton and Sons and possibly at Castelbianco are involved, since we know that they both have connections with the Vauxhall car. I'm thinking that a second visit to Stratton and Sons might be worthwhile –

61

last time Alex spoke only to the workshop foreman. I shall have to think of a suitable ruse for making the visit."

"Here we go again, Melpomene – all I can do is once more warn you to be very careful! We're dealing with extremely naughty men here you know! By the way, we've had the company checked out and it looks as though it is a genuine engineering business, but not a very busy one. Perhaps Mr Stratton and Signor Griguolo are generating income in other ways as well – as Alex rightly said, small enterprises like this are sometimes used as fronts for criminal activities."

"I'll let you know what, if anything, I do, Jimmy – I've got one or two fictional roles in mind – an elderly flower-seller or a gas inspector hardly seem appropriate this time, and I'm rather sick of being an estate agent, too, but I'll think of something!"

"Don't forget that you are a genuine Special Constable, Mel, with all the uniform – not that I can suggest how you could use it this time. Best of luck, keep me in the picture!"

Melpomene spoke to the others, telling them about the acrostic and about her latest idea to visit Stratton and Sons, "But it must be lunchtime by now, surely – shall we go out or eat something here?"

Marjorie said, "We've been talking about this, and if it suits you, Mel, we two will go and get one of our picnic lunches – give me any specific requests and I'll make a list or just get a general selection. But before we go, Mel, let me draw your attention to that brochure on the front desk that came this morning from Carson and Middleton, the office suppliers – it might give you some ideas."

It certainly did, and after everyone had satisfied their cravings with cheeses, pâté de foie gras, pickles and a selection of crusty breads, the Riley headed for Hackney, Alex driving and Melpomene supplied with a folder full of stationery items.

Alex parked round the corner, and Mel, dressed smartly in a business skirt and jacket with a white collar and wearing high heels, walked to the Stratton building and rang the bell. This time a woman emerged from a door on the left of the loading bay and said, "Yes, Madam, can I help you?"

"My name is Henrietta Musgrave, I'm visiting all the firms in this area and talking to them about ways of promoting their businesses. Would it be possible to speak to the manager, or whoever looks after advertising?"

"Please step into the office and take a seat, Miss Musgrave, and I'll see whether Mr Stratton will see you. He has a visitor with him at the moment, but I don't think he will be long."

She went to a glass-panelled door and knocked. The door opened almost at once, and a man in a business suit, with oiled black hair reaching to his collar, sidled out, turning and talking to someone beyond him in the room, saying, "Right-oh, Charles, I'll let Gian Carlo know as soon as he's back from Southampton."

The invisible Charles replied, "Thanks Grig, look forward to hearing from you! What is it, Miss Johnson, I'd like a stiff drink before I see anyone else!"

"It's a lady called Henrietta Musgrave, from some advertising company, Mr Stratton – will you see her, or shall I tell her you are not available?"

"Oh, all right, wheel her in, let's see what she's selling!"

Mel approached him and extended her hand, which he took rather limply, while indicating she should sit. "I take it that you have control of every aspect of your business, Mr Stratton – I believe that I can offer you some improvements which will enhance it. Could I trouble you to show me some of your stationery, first of all? Invoices, quotations, that sort of thing – and envelopes too. Thank you – I see. Let me guess – you haven't made any changes to these layouts for some time, is that right?"

"Yes, we have been using these forms quite successfully since my father started the company – before the war, that was. I took it over about six years ago."

"I thought as much, Mr Stratton! If you will excuse me saying so, these documents give a somewhat dated impression, due to the typeface used and the layout. You will find that some of your competitors have gone for a much more lively and eye-catching style. If you like, I can get our designers to put together a set of forms, envelopes and so on that will look modern. Do you advertise in trade publications, Mr Stratton? We can produce some samples for you in several sizes. All of this will be completely without obligation – we will give you firm quotations, if you decide to take advantage of our offer."

Chapter 22

Before she left Stratton's office, Melpomene gave him a business card – not her own, of course, but one from Carson and Middleton's, which had been included in the advertising material sent to Crabbe and Crabbe.

"I'll make sure some samples are sent to you, Mr Stratton. When you telephone, ask for Miss Musgrave – if I'm out of the office, which is often the case, please leave a message and I'll get back to you. A pleasure talking to you, sir, good day."

Back at the Riley, she found Alex almost dozing over a newspaper, but when she got in and sat down, he brightened up and said, "A few minutes after you went to Stratton's, Mel, I caught sight of the famous green Armstrong Siddeley! It must have been parked down the street, and then it drove off quite fast – I could see there were two men in it, but I didn't get a good look at them."

"I can have a guess at the name of one of them, Alex, because he left the building just as I was being shown into Stratton's office. Stratton addressed him as 'Grig' so it's odds-on that he is the engineer, Griguolo, mentioned by the foreman last time we were here. And, what's more, Alex, this supposed Griguolo alluded to 'Gian Carlo' – who could very possibly be the late Serotti's erstwhile smuggling partner, Signor Passarella! And to add to all this, Griguolo has long black hair, so there's a chance that he was the one who did the shooting, presumably to prevent Serotti from testifying – maybe the driver's death was just an unfortunate accident for the poor man. "

Alex started the car and drove off, still ruminating on all this fresh evidence, and said, "You know where we should concentrate our attention next, Mel – Castelbianco's. Didn't that foreman say I should try there if I wanted to talk to Griguolo? It's not clear whether they are a customer of Stratton's or an associate company or what. In case you're contemplating a repeat of your recent performance, Mel, I would strongly recommend against it. If this Grig should happen to spot you, he could easily put two and two together and get five – we mustn't fall into the trap of thinking that because these people are crooks, they must also be stupid – far from it, I should say! The safest way would be for me to do the approach to

Castelbianco's. Maybe we should talk to Jimmy first – he could have some bright ideas, he usually does."

"I'll do it as soon as we get back to the agency, Alex – Jimmy will be interested in what I just learnt."

So Melpomene telephoned Mile End Road police station, but finding that Jimmy was out, spoke to Cec Thomson instead.

"Did Jimmy tell you we had someone staking out the Preston house?" he said, "We've found that Signora Cinzia only does her tutoring at the embassy on Tuesdays and Thursdays, so we got a WPC in civilian clothes to follow her – at a safe distance – last Wednesday, which was somewhat of a dead loss, because she just behaved like any other housewife and went to the grocer and the butcher. But when WPC Dulcie Jarvis repeated the exercise this morning it was more entertaining. Cinzia went by tube and foot to the bank on the ground floor of the Castelbianco building – it's called 'Banca Popolare Di Palermo'. She was there for only a few minutes, while WPC Jarvis waited a few yards away, and then she came out of the bank and immediately turned into the entrance of Castelbianco's. Dulcie Jarvis scuttled after her, but was only able to spot her getting into the lift – the directory by the side of the lift doors lists Castelbianco as occupying the third to the fifth floors, and she could see from the indicator that Cinzia got out on the fourth floor. She didn't think she should follow her, and simply waited in the street. Cinzia didn't emerge for over an hour, and then went more or less straight home, but carrying a thick document folder that she didn't have earlier. That's it – end of that story, for the moment!"

"Has anyone seen anything of Mr Preston, Cec?" asked Melpomene, "It would be nice to know what part, if any, he plays in all this intrigue."

"Unfortunately, we could only spare one officer to keep watch, so when, this morning, Cinzia and her husband left the house together, she could only keep an eye on both of them up to the point when they parted in front of the tube station, deciding on the spot that Cinzia would be the one to follow. Dulcie was able to see that Preston set off up the street at a brisk walk, but of course then she had to turn her attention back to Cinzia – I told you about that already. When Jimmy returns to the station, I'll have a yarn with him about whether it will be worthwhile tagging both of them – we don't really know how important they are at this stage."

"Thanks for all that, Cec – could you ask Jimmy to telephone us when he has the opportunity – we want to discuss our next tactics with him."

"Of course, Mel, could I give him an idea about what you have in mind?"

"We've started to think about following up leads to a certain Signor Griguolo – first name not yet known – who is said to be Stratton's chief engineer, as well as a whisper about Gian Carlo Passarella, who seems to be an associate of his and is already suspected of being involved in gun-running, along with the late unlamented Angelo Serotti."

Melpomene thanked Cec Thomson and asked him to tell Jimmy that she and Alex would be going home soon, as it was getting on for dinner time. In the car, Alex said, "I've been thinking about Castelbianco's and wondering how we could find out more – it seems increasingly likely that it is a cover for clandestine operations. I would dearly like to know what part Cinzia Preston is playing, not to mention Griguolo and Passarella."

"It seems," said Mel, "that Gian Carlo Passarella is a very active operator, but it's quite likely that the real brains working behind the scenes are outwardly respectable business men, with senior, even managerial posts in the company. You remember that helpful clerk at Old Street post office, particularly the directory he showed us – 'Who Owns Who' – we were only interested in Perrin and Wesley when we there last, but we could go back there and look up Castelbianco's now. But that's a job for tomorrow, I think, I'm fairly tired now after all that acting!"

"Me too, Mel – mainly from a lot of telephoning. I'm looking forward to putting my feet up after dinner and catching up with the papers, and I assume you've dropped behind with The Times crosswords! I wonder what Mrs M is going to present us with for dinner?"

"Something solid, I hope! Lunch was nice but only a picnic."

Mrs Mountain must have read Mel's mind – it was pot roast, followed by spotted dick and custard!

Chapter 23

As they had decided, Melpomene and Alex headed for the Old Street Post Office first thing after breakfast. The helpful man who they had spoken to before was not at the reference desk, but they found an equally obliging woman in attendance.

"We looked at a directory called 'Who Owns Who' last time we were here," said Alex, "may we peruse it again?"

The woman glanced along the shelves behind her counter and said, "It's not here, I'm afraid, let me check my loans register – we sometimes lend our directories out to customers who have been approved. As you might imagine we lost a few copies before we started doing this, let me see – ah, I was right, a copy of 'Who Owns Who' was checked out an hour ago by a gentleman from the Italian Embassy – he said he would bring it back in an hour or two, so it might be worth your while to wait. Have you any other enquiries to make?"

"Yes, we want to look up some firms in the business directories. We could go over there and use the table, if that's all right."

"Here you are, then – this one covers the City, and the fat one is a general directory for the Greater London area, but not as detailed. I'll let you know when the Italian gentleman comes back with 'Who Owns Who'."

"Thank you very much, but don't point us out to him please, we don't want to get into long conversations, and we've found that Italians tend to be rather chatty!"

In the City directory, they turned first to the entry for Castelbianco SpA, and soon found a listed staff member whose name – Angelo Serotti – was already familiar to them. He was listed amongst a group of 'technical representatives', along with an entry that caused Alex to whistle and Melpomene to clap her hands before she could control herself. The name was 'Osvaldo Griguolo'!

"That confirms a conjecture that I have been developing for some time," said Alex, "that when someone devises an alias for themselves, they cling onto some part of their real name. For example, you, my dear, when you are playing a part, often call yourself 'Henrietta Musgrave' – your second Christian name and your maiden name, and I sometimes call myself 'Alan' instead of 'Alex'. I wouldn't mind betting, and I suppose you'll agree with me, that 'Osvaldo Griguolo' must really be Scarletta!"

"Yes, Alex, perhaps Griguolo is his Mama's surname. We had better keep our heads down when anyone comes in here, just in case, although it's unlikely that it will be him who's looking up stuff in 'Who Owns Who'. Meanwhile, let's see what else we can find. Did you make a note of the other companies that have come up?"

Alex looked into his notebook, "Yes, here we are Mel – Prescott Brothers, and Ward-Normandie Holdings, both mentioned by Jimmy's contact at the Fraud Squad, CI Saunders. Let's see what details we can turn up here. Not much on Prescott's – to the unaided eye this looks like a perfectly normal transport company, with a couple of levels of management, a purchasing officer and a transport supervisor, as well as unnamed office staff."

"What about Ward-Normandie?" asked Mel, "Anything interesting to us – any names we've met before?"

"No, pretty much as you might expect, once more. The only officers singled out with names, are a group of three or four called 'company liaison managers'. I suppose they deal with the subsidiaries, since this is a holding company. No names we've come across earlier, but, as you might expect from an international organization, some of the names are foreign, J-C Dupuis, F. Schleswigger, B.G. Sanantonio, for instance. I'm making notes of all the names I find, for later checking with Jimmy and his boys."

Melpomene tugged at his sleeve and nodded toward the reference desk, where a tall youngish man in a smart suit was handing back a volume. The librarian took it and checked it off against her list, and, as the man turned away, waved and lifted her thumb to Alex.

Mel said, "Excuse me a moment, Alex, I think I will try to see where this man is going once he leaves – I could be some time, but stay here and do your research and I'll come back to tell you. He doesn't look fierce, but I have my Beretta with me, loaded and ready to cock, just in case."

She walked away from the reference section into the main public area, and was just in time to see her quarry leaving by the street door. It was raining now, so the man she was following hurried along as close to the shop-fronts as possible, taking advantage of those few who had awnings. Mel did the same, a few yards back, until he darted up a side street. When she reached the corner, she peered cautiously round it and saw that the street was now empty. Thinking that he must have turned again, Mel broke into a trot and headed to the next corner, but as she was passing a doorway to a building, the man jumped out and grabbed her by the arm so hard that it was painful.

"Why are you following me, Miss? I spotted you as soon as you stepped into the street, so don't try to tell me you weren't! I've seen you before somewhere – you're a police nark, aren't you?"

Mel put on her best Cockney accent and shrieked, "I ain't got no idea what you're goin' on abaht, Mister, can't a girl try to get 'ome before she gets soaked? What's your gime, eh, I ain't got nuffink worth pinching, so you can let go of me arm – you're 'urting me!"

This tirade set the man back somewhat, so he let go of Mel's arm, which she proceeded to rub with her other hand, wincing convincingly, and then she carried on, "I've a good mind to set the coppers on to you – I ain't a nark, but they knows me all right! I could get you done for bodily 'arm, so I could!"

Just than Alex appeared round the corner, and Mel shouted to him, "Help me, Mister, this bloke is trying to rob me – he's already bruised me arm somefink cruel!"

At that, the man decided that discretion was the better part of valour and took off down the street – not running but striding out pretty fast.

Alex regarded his wife with an expression that mingled concern, humour and disapprobation, and said, "One of these days your spirit of adventure is going to land you in real trouble, my darling!"

"Nevertheless, Alex dear, it occasionally pays off!" and she presented him with a wallet and a bundle of papers, "While he was distracted I used my free hand to rifle the side pocket of his jacket, he was pressing himself against me so as not to release his grip as I wriggled to get away. There may not be anything incriminating there, but we won't know till we look!"

"You'll be the death of me, Melpomene!" exclaimed Alex.

Chapter 24

"You can't just go around picking pockets, Mel! We don't even know that this man is a crook, even though he was a bit aggressive to you!"

"You're quite right, Alex," said Melpomene, "I was rather impulsive I suppose, as a reaction to being grabbed! I tell you what – let's go back to the car and see what the wallet and his notes tell us, and then we can take steps to get his property returned to him, like responsible citizens – all right?"

Sitting back in the Riley, which was parked in a side-street, Mel, making sure they were not being overlooked, took out the contents of the wallet – a driving licence, in the name of Antonio Pellegrini, endorsed 'Diplomatic' and with the address of the Italian Embassy, several business cards with similar details, £28 in English notes and a 5000 lire Italian note, and a small photograph of a smiling woman wearing an angora beret and a white cardigan.

The bundle of papers looked like typewritten copies of entries from 'Who Owns Who', referring not only to Castelbianco and its owner, Ward-Normandie, but to several other firms, apparently in the same conglomerate. Alex made notes of their names and affiliations, as well as of Pellegrini's details, then turned to Melpomene and said, "So what do we do with these, Mel?"

"Let's go back into the Post Office and talk to that attendant at the reference desk. Maybe she has a telephone number for him in her loans register."

That indeed turned out to be the case – so Mel handed the wallet and papers to the obliging woman, saying, "That Italian gentleman dropped these in the street – could you telephone the embassy and let them know that you are holding his wallet and papers to be collected? I hope this is not too much trouble, but we were rather concerned that he should recover his property. If he wants to know, my name is Yvonne Herbison, of Chiswick. Thank you so much!"

As they walked back to the car, Alex said, "Yvonne Herbison – where on earth did that name come from?"

"Oh, I just wanted to challenge your ideas about constructing an alias, Alex – I have no more notion than you where it came from! I don't think I've ever known any Yvonnes! Let's go straight to the office, Alex my love, I'm in dire need of tea and jam tarts!"

At the office, Winnie greeted them with the news that DI Manley had some news for them, "He said to ring him before 11 and he would tell you what he'd learnt about some people who might be of interest to you. And there was also a call from Mademoiselle Deslarges in France – she didn't say what about – I suppose she doesn't yet know how much Marjorie and I can be trusted. Tea and jam tarts first?"

Over refreshments, Melpomene asked Marjorie to get Jimmy Manley on the telephone.

"Before you tell me your news, Jimmy, we found out something interesting about the legendary Osvaldo Scarletta – we reckon that he is the same man as Signor Griguolo, who Stratton said was his engineer, but is really a 'technical representative' at Castelbianco's, like the late Angelo Serotti."

"Well, Melpomene, you've scooped me on that one – I was going to tell you the same, which is very interesting and could be important – but I've got much more for you! We've tracked down Cinzia's common-law husband, going by the name of Mervyn Preston. After her successful pursuit of Cinzia, WPC Jarvis turned her attention to her partner the next time he left the house, which was yesterday afternoon. She followed him to the tube station, where he took a train – fortunately, being on duty, she didn't need to buy tickets because she had no idea where he was headed. He went to Liverpool Street, and then walked through to the main line station where he waited under the clock, would you believe! These people must be reading too many magazine romances! Anyway, after a few minutes, Preston was approached by a woman wearing a hat with a feather in it, high heels and a fur coat. They had a brief chat, then went to the waiting-room café and settled down with cups of tea for a long and intense conversation. Dulcie Jarvis wasn't able to get close enough to eavesdrop, but she could see that Preston passed the woman something fairly small but seeming to be heavy, which she immediately put into her handbag, looking furtively around to see whether she was being watched, but not noticing Dulcie, who was busying herself with coffee and a buttered tea-cake at the time."

"So that was all, was it, Jimmy?" said Melpomene, rather disappointed.

"No it wasn't, Mel – in fact I'm putting in a strong recommendation that WPC Jarvis be promoted to Detective-Sergeant because of what she did next! Mervyn Preston exchanged a few more words with the woman and then left, asking her to pay for the teas, which she did, taking some coins from her handbag that she'd put on the counter. Dulcie was standing next to her at the cash register, waiting to pay too. And then she managed to clumsily knock the handbag to the floor, and quickly bent to pick it up, muttering apologies. She was still acting clumsy, and managed to tip the contents of the bag all over the floor, including that small heavy object, which she made sure to pick up. And then she recognised it – it was a Beretta pistol – just like the one you carry, Mel – so she held on to it!"

"How did the woman react?" asked Mel.

"Dulcie expected her to be angry, but instead she reached out her hand, saying 'please give it to me, Miss!' and looked almost distressed, even close to tears. 'I'm a police officer,' said Dulcie, showing her warrant card, 'and I have to ask you this – why are you carrying this firearm and do you have a licence for it'. Then the woman began a very confused and loud explanation, so Dulcie told her she would have to come to the Kings Cross police station for a proper interview. For a moment it looked as though she was going to make a dash for it, but then she shrugged and went quietly – the bystanders were beginning to crowd round. So she was handed over to the Kings Cross boys and we shall hear the outcome in due course. By that time WPC Jarvis was more than ready to hand over and go back to her own station. I shall buy her a drink the first chance I get!"

"What an interesting story, Jimmy! We are gradually finding out more and more. By the way, could you see if there's anything on file about a gentleman called Antonio Pellegrini? We think he is from the Italian Embassy, and we encountered him at the Old Street Post Office when we and he separately were looking up details in a directory called 'Who Owns Who'. He obviously had a guilty conscience, because when I tried to shadow him he grabbed me in a very unpleasant way. I put him off by impersonating a very common person! I'll tell you on another occasion how we got hold of his details!"

Chapter 25

Alex, of course, had been listening to all this on the extension, so he and Melpomene between them told Winnie and Marjorie the story. When they had finished they each had another cup of tea, and then Winnie reminded them about the call from Mlle Deslarges, "She left a number, interestingly enough it looks like a London one – I assumed she was calling from France before – so should I ring her now?"

Mel spoke first to a woman whose voice she didn't recognize, who said, "Metropolitan Police Special Unit, here, who would you like to speak to? Mademoiselle Deslarges? Oh yes, she is here, just a moment."

Hortense was very happy to hear from Mel, saying, "*Bonjour Madame!* Are you back in your bureau now? I would very much like to pay a visit to you there soon, if that would be agreeable to you. I have a car and driver at my disposal, and I'm told he knows your address, so with your permission I will see you – and Alex too, I hope – within half an hour. If you are busy now, I can of course come later – *à bientôt!*"

As promised, Mlle Deslarges rang the front door-bell twenty minutes later. She was accompanied by a police driver, who waited to see her welcomed in by Marjorie, then tipped his cap and left.

Melpomene was not quite sure what Hortense would look like, but had constructed a mental image of a tall, chic, soignée, dark-haired woman. In the flesh, she was quite different – rather short, with an untidy mane of auburn hair and a pale complexion and hazel eyes to suit, nevertheless still chic.

She came forward and approached Mel, saying, "You must be Melpomene – Hugo said you had fair curls! And this shy gentleman has to be Alex! I'm so happy to meet you both – and your staff, too! Let me guess – the tall one is Marjorie and the other is Winnie, am I right?"

"Nearly right, Mademoiselle!" said Winnie, "Would you like some tea or coffee? If so, I'll bring it through to the back office."

As Alex ushered her through to sit down in a chair near the table, Hortense said, with a nod towards Winnie's back, "She has some spirit, that one!"

Alex said, "They are both treasures, Hortense, we are very fortunate to have them instead of mere clerks who need to be told what to do all the time! Quite the reverse – they sometimes tell us what we're supposed to be doing!"

Melpomene nodded her agreement and asked, "We're very happy to make your acquaintance, Hortense, but I'm sure this is more than a social visit – and we have some questions for you as well. You first, but have some of your tea before you start – I see Winnie has guessed that you might like Lapsang Souchong – did she get that right?"

"She did – I'm starting to see what you mean about your assistants, Melpomene, is Winnie psychic, perhaps? And I find that these little tarts of confiture are very nice too, so I will waste no time in polishing them off! But you are right about the purpose of my visit – I don't know how much you know about our current activities to do with illegal currency transfers, so I will relate to you the whole saga – for saga it is becoming."

"We've had some anecdotes from Hugo, Hortense," said Mel, "but these have concentrated on the smuggling of guns and drugs – we have a certain Osvaldo Scarletta in our sights, who interestingly was brought to our attention by a client in what seemed to be quite another connection."

"Ah yes, I know something of that person, which I will elaborate upon in a while. But I should first make a very important point to you – you may already appreciate this, but I will describe it anyway. My principal activities are in a field which is becoming referred to as 'forensic accountancy', a term which refers to the detection of embezzlement, fraud and, particularly in my case, of illicit money transfers. You will readily understand that every transaction in drugs, firearms or other illicit goods must be matched by payments. So if there is a consignment of, say, drugs, from Marseilles to London, there must be a flow of money in the reverse direction. In order to conceal these transactions, the money flow takes an entirely different route from that of the drugs. This is where I have been focussing my attention."

"And Scarletta is involved in this as well as the actual gun running?" asked Mel, "Hugo Palance told us he was going to ask you about him. He has popped up several times in our enquiries. Did you also discover that he has an alias, as Griguolo? In effect he has a dual identity – Osvaldo Scarletta

74

works under one of the commercial attachés at the Italian embassy, and his doppelgänger, Osvaldo Griguolo, is an employee of Castelbianco's, as a technical representative, whatever that is. He also seems to have a role as the chief engineer of Stratton and Sons – quite a versatile guy, our Osvaldo!"

"This is very interesting to me also," said Hortense, "from my point of view, he is involved not only in the physical transport of firearms and drugs, but in the very effective manipulation of bank accounts as well. There is a wide range of stratagems that can be used to muddy the waters of banking transactions, but M'sieu Scarletta or Griguolo seems to have invented new ones that I have only just begun to understand."

Just then, the telephone rang in the front office, and Marjorie tapped on the door, saying, "Excuse me, but Mademoiselle Deslarges is wanted on the telephone – I think it is an overseas call."

Hortense murmured an apology and went to answer it. She left the connecting door open, and the others could hear what sounded like an excited conversation conducted at a high volume, not in French, but in Italian, culminating in an exasperated exclamation by Hortense and the words "*Il dio ci aiuta tutti!*" The telephone was slammed down and Hortense came back in and sat down again.

"I do not believe this!" she said, "The Italian authorities in Roma have just demanded that we at La Sûreté hand over any information that we might be holding for a list of Italian nationals, including Signor Scarletta, that they recited to me over the telephone, and that they will telegraph a confirmatory copy of this list to our headquarters in the next few hours. I shall, of course, not comply until I have received verification at a high level in the French ministry."

Alex said, "Can you give us any idea of the reasons behind this request, Hortense? It certainly sounds very high-handed to me – have there been any earlier tensions between you at the Sûreté and your opposite numbers in Rome? Or is this the result of some recent incident?"

"I have no idea, M. Alex, I have had nothing but willing cooperation till now – I am on friendly terms with two or three officials there."

Chapter 26

Melpomene was concerned about the setback, "Is there any chance of appealing this decision – and who could do anything? It seems that this is at governmental level, and might need someone with a great deal of influence to do any good. Does the international police organization that's currently in process of formation have any clout, yet?"

"I doubt that it does, I'm afraid," said Hortense, "I hear from my colleagues that there is even some lingering resistance to it within the countries involved, by certain of the established police forces, for instance."

"We shall just have to wait and see," said Melpomene, "meanwhile, Hortense, we wanted to see whether you could help us with some Italian-sounding names we have turned up recently. Besides the man you've already given us a lot of information about, Scarletta *alias* Griguolo, there is Cinzia Preston, née Tagliamonte, and her husband, Mervyn – most likely Preston is an alias, too. Jimmy Manley has had each of these followed by one of his policewomen, with some interesting outcomes, and it would be good to know whether you at the Sûreté have any information on them."

Hortense pondered a little, and took a notebook from her handbag, "Let me see – the name Tagliamonte does ring a small bell with me, oh yes, here it is – but the Tagliamonte I have listed is a man, Benvenuto, who we picked up in Bordeaux in a raid on a drug gang. According to my notes he was given a jail sentence of ten years, which means he must still be in custody – if I may use your telephone I can check up on this quite quickly. Excuse me, I will ask one of your assistants to make the call – no doubt they understand what is needed for an overseas connection."

She went into the outer office, and Mel and Alex didn't try to eavesdrop, but took out the notes from 'Who Owns Who' that they had made at Old Street post office, as well as the summary that Alex had made of Pellegrini's papers from the same source.

"It'll save us time if we just show these to Hortense," said Alex, "of course, there may be nothing in them that will interest her."

Then, Hortense finished her call and came back.

"A certain degree of success!" she announced, "As I hoped, Benvenuto Tagliamonte is still safely under lock and key in Bordeaux, but I was also able to discover that Signorina Cinzia is his sister and sometime confederate – they were both picked up and fined some years ago, when they were still at school in Torino, for a comparatively trivial series of thefts from classmates. Cinzia would romance a boy, and Benvenuto would go through his pockets while he was distracted. They would then switch roles to rob girls. They never got away with much more than small change and things like fountain pens – they have aimed higher since moving to France!"

"How fascinating!" said Melpomene, "Presumably Cinzia has kept her nose comparatively clean since then, with a short lapse into shop-lifting. But working at the embassy and her alliance with Preston must have presented her with further temptations."

Alex added, "This collaboration is proving very worthwhile, Hortense, thank you very much! There is also a man called Antonio Pellegrini, who we had an encounter with recently, but maybe he's on the Italian government's protected list. That is possibly also the case with Gian Carlo Passarella, who seems to be an associate of Griguolo. Mel overheard a conversation at Stratton and Sons in which he was mentioned, when she was pretending to be the representative of a printing company. His name also turned up as someone who was detained with cocaine in his luggage, in company with the late Angelo Serotti, and subsequently deported on the request of the Naples authorities, who alleged he was a member of the Camorra. He has apparently extricated himself, possibly by bribery, and returned to London – we intercepted a coded letter to Serotti that had his fingerprints on it."

"But," said Melpomene, "can we leave all that until after lunch, please? I'm feeling rather peckish already – perhaps, Hortense, with your Italian connections, you might like to sample the fare at Guiseppe's, our favourite trattoria?"

The lunch was indeed enjoyed by all, enlivened by some badinage in Sicilian between Hortense and their waiter, whose origins she had identified by his accent. He was entranced to find someone who was comfortable in his dialect, and this probably enhanced the quality of his waiting, and persuaded him to present them, on the house, with a bottle of Inzolia, a white wine that none of them had met before. It was with some reluctance that they made their way back to the agency – as Alex remarked, it was a good thing that they had made their way to Guiseppe's by foot.

They put their heads together over the list of names that had been put together. Hortense could supply details for some of them, and promised to look others up once she was back in Paris.

"And besides," she said, "I will make a through exploration of the files that Adrian Fitz-Hugh and his people have collated, while I'm in London. I have a colleague in the unit called Mario Donizzetti, who has paid particular attention to French and Italian suspects, especially Scarletta, and I'm looking forward to working with him again after a break of three or four years. We were fairly close when I was working in Rome for a while. Now I have a question for you two – do you know of a reliable accountant who could collaborate with me in investigating some of these London companies that have come to our notice? I could make enquiries myself, of course, but I thought you may have someone you could recommend."

"We certainly have such a contact, Hortense," said Melpomene, "he has worked with us twice before and he seems very acute and competent. His name is Philip Seaward, and he audited the books of the St Luke Embassy after all the trouble we discovered there, as well as tracking down illicit financial practices at a hospital we were investigating – he's clearly au fait with forensic accounting. I'll get Marjorie or Winnie to give you his details and telephone number – of course, feel free to mention our names."

"Perhaps you could call him for me, Melpomene, rather than have me explain myself from scratch," said Hortense, "but I could approach him myself if you prefer. Now, I know you are a solicitor, Alex, but maybe it would also be good for me to have the name of an advocate – a barrister, I suppose, in the English system – who you could recommend, in case we are successful enough to get some of these characters into court. I'm sure that the big villains will have access to high-priced lawyers if it ever gets to this point!"

"Once again we can help!" said Alex, "Archie Staples, who has worked with us before, is a KC – I suppose you know the significance of this qualification, Hortense. Once again, Marjorie and Winnie can give you his details."

Chapter 27

Hortense had another comment, "You have mentioned your original client in this case a couple of times, but I'm not sure how and where everything fits – I think it might be helpful if you could relate the outline of the whole story to me, so that I can better see how it all goes together – I realize that there are still gaps, here and there."

Melpomene said, "What a good suggestion, Hortense – this makes me think that a chart might help. I should explain that my training is in the field of social anthropology, and we have often found that constructing sociograms or similar networks has helped us sort out some of our more complex cases. Marjorie – have we still got some of those big sheets of cartridge paper?"

"Yes, Mel, and there's plenty of coloured pencils, too. Shall I lay some out on the table here?"

"I'll start by drawing a little box for our initial client, Philomena Hotchkiss. She came to us worried that her husband Eric had become very moody, and that she thought it was because of what was happening in his workplace, the brokerage firm Perrin, Wesley and Associates – you've heard us speak about them, Hortense. So I'll draw a box for them, and then little branches to ones for Osvaldo and Ronald Sedgwick, two of the people who were harassing Eric, I'll colour them red to indicate that they are potential enemies, maybe even crooks. And over this side we'll have the goodies at Perrin and Wesley – Liz Purvis, Eric's secretary, and Beryl Sykes, the office manager, I'll colour them green."

Melpomene carried on expanding her chart, commenting to Hortense on each new entry. Soon she had boxes for Castelbianco's, Stratton and Sons and the other firms that had been mentioned by the Fraud Squad and by Hortense herself, who, by this time was becoming quite involved in the whole process, making suggestions and pointing out links.

Then Winnie came in and said, "It's getting quite late – do you want Marjorie and me to stay, or can we go home now – don't work too long yourselves or you'll be fit for nothing in the morning!"

This prompted Hortense to say, "Quite right, Mlle. Winnie, I'll come back tomorrow if Melpomene and Alex can put up with me. Could you ring for my car, please?"

"Oh," said Alex, "don't bother your driver, Hortense – Mel and I will run you home – where are you staying?"

"Hang on a moment," said Melpomene, "let me ring the flat and find out what Mrs Mountain is preparing for our dinner – if it's something you like, Hortense, you're very welcome to join us."

She went to the telephone, had a brief conversation and reported back, "You're in luck, Hortense, our meal tonight is a traditional English dish you might not have had a chance to sample before – Lancashire Hotpot – are you willing to take a chance? And there's jam roly-poly with custard to follow – I don't suppose you've met that in France or Italy! And we can accompany that with a bottle of our favourite Côtes du Rhône, to add a French touch!"

"This is *trés gentil* of you – I will risk it!" replied Hortense, "I am anyway an adventurous person!"

Melpomene drove the Riley to the flat, the furniture and décor of which charmed Hortense, who said, "I had formed the impression that English interior design lacked flair in general, so I'm happy to see that you two have achieved a fine balance between the traditional and modern. I particularly like your Art Deco wireless set, this is in a style that is *au courant* without being *avant-garde*!"

And, of course, they all enjoyed the meal, which was up to Christabel Mountain's usual standard, and afterwards settled down to some relaxed conversation, studiously avoiding shop talk.

"What do you do to make a break from work, Hortense?" asked Alex, "I'm a golf fan myself, but I'm not able to play as much as I would like."

"As for me," she replied, "I am an enthusiastic skier – I try to make room for at least two weeks every year – a couple of months ago I had an enjoyable ten days in Cortina d'Ampezzo with a good friend, Commissario Nicolo Fonzi, from the Questura in Venice – we made a compact that we would not discuss police work while we were there. And beside *le ski*, I am an admirer of old porcelain – by the time I retire I hope to have built an impressive collection. How about you, Melpomene?"

"I do play tennis from time to time – there are courts at my family's hotel in the south of England, and, like Alex, I enjoy music, but am no performer, which I regret – in English we say that I have cloth ears! We both enjoy good music, both in the concert hall and over the wireless. We've tried gramophone records, but it's too frustrating to have one's listening enjoyment broken into three-minute pieces! Otherwise, I am addicted to crossword puzzles – I gather that these are not as popular in France as they are here, somehow – perhaps French is too precise, whereas it is the English tendency towards ambiguity and jokiness that makes it fit for cryptic crosswords. I tell Alex that solving these is good practice for keeping the analytical mind in tune."

"Talking about music and the wireless," said Alex, "we should look in this new magazine, the Radio Times, to see whether there is anything appealing being broadcast this evening. Let me see, what's the time? Ah yes, we're in luck, after the nine o'clock news there is a piano recital by Dame Myra Hess and Irene Scharrer, including one of my favourites, Fauré's Dolly Suite, so, Hortense, you will be able to hear some French music if you would like to!"

"That would be splendid – how did you arrange this, chér Alex? Do you have influence with the BBC?"

"That would be nice, but I'm afraid not! Shall we listen to the news first?"

After the wireless warmed up, they heard the familiar announcement, '*This is London calling. It is nine o'clock and here is the news. There has been an unprecedented drop in the prices of certain financial shares, following the announcement by the London Stock Exchange of the arrest of members of the board of a prominent company and the suspension of trading in its shares. A spokesman told our reporter that this was not expected to signal a general movement as only the one firm was involved directly, but there could be some ramifications. And now for some football results. League, Division 1: Accrington Stanley 3, Wolverhampton Wanderers 2; …*'

Alex turned down the volume, saying, "We can wait for the details in The Times tomorrow morning! Interesting, though, don't you think – wonder if it's any of our firms? Now, let's listen to our concert, it should be on now."

Chapter 28

The concert turned out to be worth sitting up for, and all three expressed their pleasure with it, Hortense saying that she was very fond of Fauré, especially his Dolly Suite, as well as the piano duets by Schubert that were also on the programme. And then she announced that she really had to be getting back to her hotel, before she fell asleep, "It's close to Scotland Yard, an easy walk to Sir Adrian Fitz-Hugh's offices. I believe you know the area so if it's not too much trouble, maybe you could drop me back there soon."

She declined the offer of a cup of hot chocolate, then Alex drove her to the hotel and made sure the foyer was still attended before dropping her, saying, "Should we come for you in the morning, Hortense – we all need to work on our chart a bit more, don't we?"

"Certainly, Alex, but after breakfast I would like to have a few words with Sir Adrian before I come to your bureau. Would ten-thirty be a good time for you to pick me up at Adrian's office?"

"Very good, Hortense, and maybe Adrian would be free for a chat with Mel and me – we could bring him up to date with what we've been doing, and vice versa! We'll bring the chart with us and see you at Sir Adrian's office at ten-thirty."

The next morning, there was something of a tussle at breakfast between Melpomene and Alex over who should read The Times first, which was won by Mel, who immediately turned to the financial pages.

"Well, there's hardly any more information than on the BBC news!" she complained, "I had hoped they would name the firms involved, but all they say is stuff like 'a prominent brokerage firm' and 'directors of an established finance house' – how disappointing, I was hoping that we might recognise some names!"

"You could probably catch Eric Hotchkiss at home at this time, Mel – why don't you give him a call and see whether he knows anything."

Philomena answered the telephone and said, "Oh, Melpomene, I suppose you heard the rumours! Eric left early today, because there's all sorts of hoo-hah going on at Perrin and Wesley since yesterday, when plain-clothes police arrived there and interviewed a number of people for an hour or more, after which two of the directors, and a couple of others whose names didn't mean much to me, and someone I certainly know only too well, Ronald Sedgwick, were escorted off the premises. So we can safely assume that the brokerage firm figuring in the news is Perrin and Wesley!"

"Thanks, Phil – we might be able to find out more later, we're going to Scotland Yard soon – if there's anything you might be interested in, we'll certainly bring you up to date."

At the arranged time, Melpomene drove into the forecourt at Scotland Yard, and was approached by a policeman wanting to know what their business was. As soon as she mentioned the name of Sir Adrian Fitz-Hugh he saluted and indicated where she could park the Riley, and they soon went into the outer office of the Special Operations group, where they were recognised and ushered into Adrian's office, to see Hortense and Adrian discussing matters with a woman who neither of them had met before.

Adrian stood as they came in, and said, "Some introductions are in order, I believe. You two know Hortense already, of course, but you will not have met Chief Inspector Patricia McMahon of the Fraud Squad, who is liaising between that body and our group. Patricia, please meet Melpomene and Alex Crabbe, the principals of a detective agency that we have collaborated with on several occasions over the past months, leading to some notable successes. Detective-Inspector Manley, who you know well, holds them in high regard, as he will readily tell you, Patricia."

"Very pleased to meet you!" said CI McMahon, "I was just telling Sir Adrian and Mlle Deslarges what we know about the current shenanigans in the City – some of it, anyway, there are always plots and counterplots going on, that's the nature of high finance, I'm afraid! We were the ones who initiated the police approach to Perrin and Wesley yesterday, and there will be more activities to come over the next days and weeks, as we follow our lines of enquiry."

"Would you feel free to divulge some names?" asked Melpomene, "We have been told that Ronald Sedgwick was one of those taken in for questioning – he was someone who was prominent in harassing our client, Eric Hotchkiss, the reason why why we were engaged by Eric's wife, Philomena in the first place. Since then we have heard a few more names of people at Perrin and Wesley who Eric thought might be involved in suspicious practices, such as a Commodore Lane, who Philomena thought was quite high up in the firm – she also felt rather dubious about a woman called Sylvia Myers, but this was just on a first impression – she had no reason to suspect her of evil-doing, she was merely obnoxious!"

Alex added, "Apart from those at P and W, we have a few names that we've already mentioned to Adrian and Hortense – Osvaldo Scarletta is the most interesting of these, since he has popped up several times in different ways."

"Well," said Patricia McMahon, "why don't I go through my notes and give you a quick run-down of anything that seems immediately relevant. Perhaps we could do this over tea or coffee, Adrian?"

"What a good idea, Pat, I'll get that organised – and I think the budget could run to some cakes or something. While we're waiting, Alex' remarks about Scarletta remind me that Hortense just handed me a fat dossier, compiled by the Sûreté in collaboration with their Italian equivalents, the Polizia di Stato as well as the Guardia di Finanza, who look after customs matters. I haven't yet had a chance to peruse it completely, but, if Hortense has no objection, I can let Alex and Melpomene have copies of any relevant sections, including those about Osvaldo Scarletta, alias Griguolo. I'll ask Thelma Harris, my p.a., to see what she can do while we're attending to Patricia's report."

When everyone was supplied with tea or coffee and their chosen cakes, Patricia McMahon began.

"As some of you already know, Ronald Sedgwick was asked to accompany our men, as also were two members of the Board, Sir William Carr-Hazelton and Felix Cattermole – would anyone like to guess his nickname around the City? And also there were two divisional managers as well as Sedgwick, Commodore Gordon Lane – known as 'Shady' – and an American, Wilson Tuckett – too dull to have a nickname apparently. After interrogation, which lasted several hours, most of them were allowed to depart, but cautioned not to leave the City nor their homes."

Chapter 29

"What puzzles me a little, Patricia," said Melpomene, "is how you go about detecting this sort of wrong-doing – I assume it involves auditing the books, so does the Fraud Squad have open access to these, or what? I imagine that firms would guard their accounts very carefully, since their business depends on the impression created with the share-buying public – is that right, or am I being rather naïve?"

"Not at all Melpomene – may I call you that? You are quite right in general terms, but of course there are complications. What we always have to start with are the company reports – there is a statutory requirement that these are regularly lodged with the Exchange, with rigidly prescribed content. Our auditors – some of our staff are professionally-qualified accountants – scrutinize sample reports. We haven't the resources to do this for every firm, so we rely on the Exchange for the bulk of the checking. Some of the reports we deal with more fully are simply chosen on a random basis, but some we pick out because we've reason to suspect something. In the case of Perrin and Wesley, we based our attack on complaints made to the Exchange, and because we had started to have bad impressions about some of the Directors, particularly Carr-Hazelton, and also about Commodore Lane, who had been charged with 'affray in company with others' over an incident in a pub, about three years ago – his barrister got him off somehow."

"Oh!" said Alex, "that brings to mind something that Philomena Hotchkiss told us happened at a social event at P&W, when she overheard Commodore Lane bragging to someone, 'I'll get some of my ex-stokers to sort these gentlemen out in a day or two, meanwhile, don't say anything' – this sounded like some sort of forcible coercion, she thought. But I'm interested in Sedgwick's arrest – what were the grounds for that, and how was he identified as a suspect? The last we heard of him, he was trying to persuade Eric Hotchkiss into some activity that was distressing him, but it didn't appear to us to be anything more than verbal bullying at that stage."

"Ronald Sedgwick has been charged with embezzlement and falsification of documents," Patricia said, "based on our initial scrutiny of the contents of his filing cabinets. My colleague who is doing this tells me that he has no doubt that further evidence will emerge after a more thorough search."

"So that's one villain taken care of!" said Melpomene.

Patricia McMahon went on, "As well as Perrin and Wesley – and some completely unrelated firms – my colleague CI Saunders has been visiting Castelbianco's regularly, ever since the name of Angelo Serotti was brought to our notice. This will ring bells with you, of course, but that man has been taken out of the picture now – we assume that he was assassinated to ensure that any information he had in his possession was not acquired by us or the regular police. As you might guess, this makes us all the more keen to make enquiries at that firm and its associated companies. DI Jimmy Manley has promised to keep me informed about the enquiries into the shooting, but I've heard nothing so far."

"Can you tell us any more about Osvaldo?" asked Melpomene, "And we wonder whether your people have recently come across Gian Carlo Passarella, who Hortense Deslarges tells us is active in smuggling guns and drugs."

"We have all the files on Passarella from the Sûreté, but we haven't been able to pursue him further, as yet. And Adrian will still give you copies of what we know about Osvaldo, as he has promised."

Sir Adrian's personal assistant entered the room and whispered in his ear, whereupon he said, "We have just had a call from DI Manley for Melpomene or Alex. Thelma will show one or both of you where to take it."

Melpomene went into the outer office and picked up the telephone, to hear Jimmy say, "I tried your office first, Mel, and Marjorie told me where I could find you. I've got some more information about the woman who met Preston at Liverpool Street, also, more importantly, about the gun that he passed to her. It was a Beretta, as I think you've been told – so our firearms experts did what they usually do, and shot off a couple of rounds into a block of wax so they could examine the markings on the bullet left by the pistol. Compared under their special microscope, they matched the one retrieved at autopsy from the driver of the Vauxhall! As for the woman, we are still baffled. She gave us a patently false name and address, so we are still holding her on a charge of carrying an unlicensed fire-arm until we can induce her to come clean. She was not carrying anything by which she might be identified, and refuses to say much, but when she bumped her hip on the corner of the table as she was being taken from the interview room, she muttered, 'porca miseria!', which doesn't sound very English!"

"What about fingerprints, Jimmy?"

"Mixed success, Mel – we took hers, of course, and they are being checked against our records, but nothing yet. We've sent photostats to the French and Italian authorities, so they might find her in their files. The other prints on the gun match Passarella's – they were also found on that coded letter sent to Serotti, so all we've got to do is find him now – we know that he was around recently, so we're keeping Castelbianco's and Stratton's under surveillance. We'd like to search the Italian Embassy, of course, but that's out of the question because of diplomatic immunity, so all we can do is watch the exits. We're also no nearer finding Preston – he never returned to his mews flat after the Liverpool Street incident, but again we have a watch out for him. It goes without saying that all the ports and airports have been alerted in case he or Passarella tries to do a bunk. I've formed the opinion that he gave the gun to that woman merely to get rid of it – though chucking it in the Thames might have been easier!"

"What about the man who had an altercation with me after our visit to Old Street post office?" asked Melpomene, "His name is Antonio Pellegrini, according to his driving licence."

"Yes, I checked him out, Mel," said Jimmy, "he seems to be a legitimate employee of the Italian Embassy, not that this automatically exonerates him – I simply rang up and asked for him by name and they found him immediately, apparently in the Trade Attaché's section. When he answered I gave no name, but simply said I was from the post office, making sure he had got his property back all right – he was happy to confirm this. But we took the precaution of looking him up and there was nothing in Criminal Records here. Maybe Hortense will find some reference in her records at the Sûreté, or in Italy – that is, if they haven't put him on their restricted list. By all means, pass all this on to the others, Mel – however I shall be sending Sir Adrian a full report as soon as it's all been typed up – you could tell him that for me, please. If our surveillance exercises produce anything interesting, of course we'll let everyone involved know. Until then, keep happy and be careful!"

Chapter 30

On their way back to the office after the meeting, Melpomene said, "We seem to be getting a great deal of information now, but we shall have to decide what action to take – we can't just wait for things to happen by themselves, can we, Alex? I would like to see if we can't get some more out of the pistol woman before she has to go to court to answer the charge of possession of an unlicensed firearm. Do you know where she is being held?"

"Jimmy would know, let's give him a call when we get back. Did you have anything in mind, Mel? I suppose she must have known Preston, and had some arrangement to meet him, so it would be good to find some way of getting her to talk – possibly by trickery, since we can't resort to torture – but she seems determined to keep silent. Maybe her fingerprints will help, if they are on file anywhere – Italy sounds a good bet, judging by her inadvertent expletive, so Hortense might be able to find something out about her through her associates there."

"Perhaps we'd be better off turning out attention back to Cinzia and Mervyn," said Melpomene, "apparently he is still on the loose, but she may have gone back to her flat – let's ring Jimmy as soon as we get to the office and get the latest – I assume that his people still have the flat under surveillance. The other thing I've been turning over in my mind is finding ways of getting into the Italian Embassy – there are obviously several people there that it would be valuable to scrutinize more closely, like Scarletta and Pellegrini – it's a pity we're not in contact with someone inside – like a file clerk or even a cleaner."

"I wonder whether they use an employment agency to recruit their short-term staff, Mel? We could enquire around the district and see what agencies there are – if the Embassy has a rapid turnover, they might have chosen to use a local firm."

"And if they have any vacancies at the moment. I could ….." mused Mel, "but I would have to change my appearance because Pellegrini would remember our encounter in some detail, I should think!"

As soon as they got to the office, Alex rang Mile End Road and spoke to Jimmy and asked him if there was any news of the Prestons.

"No, Alex, Mervyn has gone to ground, nobody knows where. Cinzia came back to their flat, but claimed she is as puzzled as we are about her husband's whereabouts. However, the PC who went there to question her noticed a couple of suitcases in the hallway, so when he left he rang here, and we sent someone to follow her – not Dulcie Jarvis, because she might be recognized, but another CID man, DC Drysdale, who has experience in working under cover. He reached the flat just in time, as she was outside getting herself and her luggage into a taxi, so he got back into the squad car that had taken him there and they proceeded to follow the taxi to Paddington station. When she paid off the taxi, she waited for a porter, so Drysdale had no trouble following her by foot to the booking office, where she bought a one-way ticket to Southampton. Drysdale made sure she actually boarded the train and then telephoned us. We already had a border watch set up for Mervyn Preston, so we simply extended it to cover her. We told the Southampton people she might be using her maiden name, Tagliamonte, and of course we gave them a description, so let's hope!"

Later, over the inevitable cups of tea and jam tarts, Marjorie and Winnie wanted to know what had been achieved at the meeting, and when Melpomene mentioned the possibility of trying to get a temporary job at the Embassy, Winnie said, "I see what you mean about not being recognised by this Pellegrini, but you are missing the obvious solution – why don't I try to get a job there? Besides anything else, I'm experienced in clerical work, whereas you, Mel, if you will forgive me for saying so, would have to bluff your way into the job without knowing what you're doing – so sooner or later you would inevitably be rumbled! What if someone were to ask you to take dictation? Or even type something up?"

Marjorie agreed, "I think Winnie would be the woman for that sort of job – but why don't I ring the Embassy and enquire about the tutor vacancy, now we know that Cinzia is gone? Perhaps they put people on without using an agency – anyway I can try to find out."

She looked up the telephone number, and when it was answered, said, "Oh, good afternoon, this is Calloway's employment agency, could you put me through to your office manager, please? – Thanks for speaking to me, Mrs Abbott – I know you usually work through another agency, but we specialise in tutors and I believe your current person has just left you, so maybe we can fill the gap? The lady we have in mind follows the immersion method of language teaching, so she will work entirely in English. I'm told that her prospective pupils have a basic grasp of the language, so they will probably progress faster than if they are tempted to fall back on Italian when they are puzzled. I suppose the parents of the young girls concerned will have the last word, and we understand this, of course. Perhaps I could ask the tutor to come to the Embassy for interview – her name is Henrietta Musgrave and she is free at the moment. Oh good, ten o'clock tomorrow morning would be fine – should she ask for you, Mrs Abbott?"

Marjorie rang off and sat down rather hurriedly, "I must be sweating like a pig!" she said, "That was rather nerve-wracking!"

"You did extremely well, Marjorie!" said Melpomene, "I'd better make you another cup of tea – sorry we've got no brandy to put in it! Now I'd better read up on this immersion method – where did you hear about it?"

"Why, from Jimmy Manley, of course! He's been studying French that way, and he swears by it! He started off at ordinary evening classes, but he says he's been shooting ahead since he switched!"

"Right oh, Marjorie, I'll give Jimmy a call now and pump him on it, and also let him know about our latest mad plan!"

But when she rang Mile End Road, Mel was told that Jimmy was tied up with an urgent job that had just come in, but that he would be asked to get back to her as soon as possible.

"Ask him to ring me at the flat, please, we'll be leaving the office very shortly."

And, as it happened, Jimmy rang up not long after Mel and Alex had just finished enjoying a sumptuous meal of 'cock-o vinny', as Mrs Mountain called it.

Melpomene answered and said, "You first, Jimmy, and then I'll tell you our news. Is it anything we'd be interested in?"

"I would think so, Melpomene – the body of a woman was discovered when the 4.15 from Paddington arrived at Southampton. There were gunshot wounds to the back of the head, and the victim's description tallies with that of Cinzia."

90

Chapter 31

Jimmy went on, "Unfortunately, the actual time and place of death is impossible to establish exactly, since all we know is that the murder happened between four o'clock, when DC Drysdale saw Cinzia boarding the train, and the time that the body was discovered at Southampton when the guard checked all the compartments – it could even have happened before the train left Paddington. A further complication is that the train stopped at Reading – the staff there have been questioned but no-one noticed her, alive or dead. She was just slumped in the corner of her seat when she was found, so anybody seeing her would probably have assumed she was asleep. We and the Reading and Southampton police will make appeals in the press and on the wireless for witnesses, but I'm not holding my breath. Be assured I'll let you know if there are any interesting results from the p.m. and the forensics – that carriage has been shunted onto a siding until our people have had a chance to go over it. Now Mel, what was it you wanted to tell me?"

"It kind of pales into insignificance now, Jimmy, but when you told us that Cinzia was trying to leave the country, we thought that it would be a clever wheeze for me to try to take her place at the embassy as English tutor to the diplomats' children. And I've actually got an appointment to discuss this with the office manager, Mrs Abbott, at ten o'clock tomorrow morning. She's been given the impression that I'm familiar with the immersion method of language teaching, so I need to have a chat with you, Jimmy – they tell me you've recently been learning French this way – is that right?"

"Very smart approach, Melpomene – judging by my experience with French you'll hardly need to speak any Italian at all, so you'll probably get away with it! What happens with our class – we're a group of about ten – is that the tutor breezes in, says 'Bonsoir tout le monde!' and launches into whatever topic he's chosen for the evening. He refuses to lapse into English even when we don't understand, just uses various forms of words in French until we tumble. I presume that you are using this stratagem as a way to infiltrate the Embassy and snoop around!"

"You're right of course, Jimmy – and if I don't get the job, Winnie is going to try to go for some sort of clerical or secretarial position there – she pointed out, quite rightly, that I wouldn't be capable of that sort of work – I can hardly type and I couldn't take dictation – Alex is the one with shorthand! Wish me luck with my interview!"

After an early breakfast, Melpomene rushed out of the flat, explaining to Alex that she was going to have something done to her hair, "And if I wear a pair of specs, that should be enough to put Pellegrini off the scent if I bump into him!"

She went to the hairdresser who had dyed her hair brown on a previous occasion, when she had become a Special Constable, but she chose not to have her curls permed out this time, simply selecting a rather fetching auburn shade from the samples offered, Just over an hour later she was back at the flat as a ravishing redhead.

"I might keep it for a while," she told Alex, "you look as though you rather fancy me like this – do you? What about my outfit, is it plain enough for a teacher? You'd better drop me some distance away from the Embassy door – a modest tutor would travel by tube, wouldn't she?"

There was a sign by the front door, listing the hours of business and inviting visitors to enter. In the lobby there was an official behind a counter, who asked her business.

"I have an appointment with Mrs Abbott." Mel told him; he picked up a telephone, spoke briefly and then said, "Someone will be along shortly to take you to her – you may sit over there if you wish."

When Mel was ushered into her office, Mrs Abbott rose and extended her hand, saying, "I do hope I can appoint you today, Mrs Musgrave – you wouldn't believe how long it took us to find Mrs Preston, and now she's up and left us, with only a few hours' notice. Perhaps you could tell me about your qualifications?"

Melpomene explained that she had a first class honours degree from the London School of Economics – without saying in what area – and went on to explain her intention to use the immersion method. To her surprise, Mrs Abbott smiled and said, "I picked up my working grasp of Italian the same way, at Regent Street Polytechnic, so I quite understand. Without further ado, I'll take you to meet your pupils – at the moment there are five of them. Apart from the English lessons, they are all working at correspondence courses from Italy in their other subjects, so that they do not drop behind too much while their parents are on post."

They went to a lift and up to the fourth floor where there was a light airy room with a blackboard, a row of desks and some settees and easy chairs. Lounging about and chattering were three girls, looking to be between eight and twelve years old, and two boys, a little younger.

"Ciao ragazzi!" said Mrs Abbott, "Here is your new English teacher, Mrs Musgrave." She went round the group, and as each child was named – Rosa Scarletta, Gabriela Ponzi, Beatrice Manfredi, and Gerardo and Rafaello Ferrero – he or she came and shook hands with Mel, adding a little bow or curtsy.

Melpomene had a good look at Rosa but said nothing more to her than the 'how d'you do' she murmured to the others. Then she addressed the class, saying, "We won't have a proper lesson today – I will talk to Mrs Abbott and we'll decide when I'll come every week. But when I see you next, you must each tell me a little bit about yourself. Arrivederci!"

Mel went back to Mrs Abbott's office to discuss timetable and payments with her, and said, "I would like to meet the parents at some time that would suit them, so that they can tell me anything that I should know about the children, and so that the parents can decide whether I'm suitable, too!"

"Leave that all to me, Mrs Musgrave," said Mrs Abbott, "please leave me your telephone number – I'll write down my direct number for you as well, so you won't always have to go through the Embassy switch. As far as I can see, you will make an excellent tutor – to tell you the truth, I had my misgivings about Cinzia Preston, she was not always very frank with me! By the way, how did you find out that she had left us?"

"The employment agency that I work through, Calloway's, told me – I really have no idea how they found out."

"Ah well, no problem – I'm just grateful we found you – or you found us! I'll talk to the attaché who has oversight of local employees and confirm the arrangements with him before I let you know – it shouldn't take more than a day or two, with any luck. I'll show you to the front door – this place is a bit of a rabbit warren, I'm afraid! Goodbye, it's been a pleasure!"

"Arrivederci, Signora!"

Chapter 32

Melpomene walked back to the side-street where Alex was waiting in the car and took her seat with a sigh of relief.

"That went off quite well," she said, "but I must admit I was a bit nervous. Fortunately, Mrs Abbott, the office manager was so anxious to replace Cinzia that I think she would have welcomed anyone who looked half-way suitable. She'll get approval from someone higher up at the Embassy and telephone me. I gave her the number of the flat, so I must prime Caroline and Mrs M, so that if anyone asks for Mrs Musgrave they will know what to say."

"Good decision!" said Alex, "We don't want to disclose our true identities to anyone who could be dubious. If you're not there when she calls, they could say they would get a message to you – without saying how – and then you can ring her."

"I wonder if there was anything about Cinzia on the news or in the papers this morning, Alex? Did you get a chance to check?"

"No, but the papers should have been delivered to the office by now – and I think the BBC has a mid-day news bulletin now, since the restrictions on day-time news broadcasts were lifted. Maybe Marjorie and Winnie have been checking – I gave them an outline on the telephone this morning, while you were at the hairdresser's. And Jimmy said he would let us know as soon as he finds out if anything interesting has turned up at the autopsy or if the forensic people find anything in the train."

They drove straight to the office, where Winnie presented them with three different newspapers, all folded back to interesting items, ranging from, 'Death on the 4.15!' (The Trumpet) to 'Unexplained Fatality' (The Times). In none of them was the identity of the victim given, merely stating that she was an apparently respectable middle-aged woman. Only The Trumpet mentioned gunshot wounds.

"No doubt we'll get more information as soon as Jimmy Manley has the results of the p.m." said Alex, and they didn't have long to wait, as the telephone rang half an hour later. Alex picked it up, and Melpomene seized the extension ear-piece.

"Doctor Phipps, at Southampton General, is sending a complete report of his autopsy to me by courier, but he told me the main points of interest." said Jimmy, "There was only one exit wound, under the chin – the murderer had wrapped her scarf around the lower part of her face to cover it up. The doctor retrieved the other bullet, still in the cranial area, which was a small calibre type, possibly from a point two-two pistol. The ballistics people are examining it so that if a gun of that sort turns up they can see whether or not it matches. This calibre is mainly used for target shooting, so I've got Cec Thomson checking discreetly whether anyone at the Embassy or at Perrin and Wesley or Castelbianco belongs to a gun club. It's not the usual sort of gun used by criminals, as a two-two hasn't got much stopping power. Dr Phipps said that the gun had probably been held against the back of her head, judging by bruising and powder burns, and she was extensively bruised around the neck and shoulders, as though she had been held tightly, by a tall burly man most likely. I think that those are the most important results of the autopsy for our purposes. As far as the forensic examination of the carriage goes, there are so many fingerprints everywhere in the compartment, as you might think, that it seems unlikely that anything useful will turn up. The second bullet hasn't been found yet."

"So unless a witness comes forward, we haven't got much chance of finding the assailant, have we?" said Melpomene, taking the receiver from Alex, "Unless we come across someone carrying a gun of that calibre. I'm a bit puzzled why such a small gun was chosen – we know that they have others at their disposal, like the one that was used to dispose of Serotti and his driver, which Preston passed to that uncommunicative woman – is she still keeping mum, Jimmy?"

"You just said, 'they', Mel, as if we were dealing with a single enemy – it's by no means certain that that is the case. Maybe the killer of Serotti and his driver has no connection with whoever bumped off Cinzia – we just don't know – if we make assumptions they might throw us off the scent."

Melpomene was still unconvinced, "We know Cinzia and Preston are connected, and we know that Preston was the one who tried to pass on the Beretta which was used in the attack on Serotti, so it seems highly likely that there is a link here, don't you think, Jimmy?"

"We're still investigating certain lines, as you know, Mel, so we ought to keep checking back. Got to go now, I'll catch up with you later."

Alex had been listening intently to this conversation, and when Jimmy rang off, said, "While we're on the subject, Mel, have you been keeping your big chart up to date? I'm wondering whether all these dramatic recent events have drawn our attention away from our original enquiry from Eric Hotchkiss – what I'm getting at is should we look more closely into the people at Perrin and Wesley he complained of initially, who were pressuring him to behave in ways that might be doubtful? Some of their names have come up since, but are there any that we have been ignoring recently?"

"Let's think," said Mel, "as I recall, the first name that Philomena mentioned was Ronald Sedgwick, Eric's superior, followed by Osvaldo. We now know that Sedgwick was arrested by the Fraud Squad and charged with embezzlement among other things, so pending his trial he's safely out of the picture. We still don't know much about Osvaldo except that he goes by two names – Scarletta at the Italian Embassy and Griguolo at Castelbianco's and Stratton and Sons'. And it looks as though his daughter, Rosa, is in my English class! But I ought to make it clear that I have no intention whatsoever of questioning her – I think that would be immoral! However, any piece of information she might drop unprompted could possibly come in useful!"

Alex said, "I applaud your resolve, Mel! But there were a couple more names raised by Eric Hotchkiss, weren't there? One I recall was someone called Peter Walsh, who was involved in the earlier claim of unprofessional conduct by Sedgwick that Archie Staples told us about, and there was also a shady solicitor called Hepworth, who might know a thing or two."

"We have some reliable friendly contacts inside Perrin and Wesley," said Melpomene, "as well as Eric himself, so it should be possible to do some quiet investigation around the firm – I wonder whether Patricia McMahon's Fraud Squad people came across anything else while they were perusing Sedgwick's filing cabinets. And in between teaching English at the Embassy, I might be able to tap into some gossip – I wonder whether an English tutor is allowed to use the same tea-room or whatever as the regular staff."

"Supposing you actually get the job, my dear! When did Mrs Abbott say she would get back to you?"

Chapter 33

Melpomene answered, "Mrs Abbott didn't actually give me a time when she would let me know – anyway, there's no particular hurry. Talking about tea-rooms reminds me that it must be getting close to lunch time – shall we go to Guiseppe's or just have something from the corner shop? Maybe we'll ask Winnie to bring us something when she gets hers – she knows what we like by now. Marjorie's Mum usually packs her lunch for her."

As it happened, Winnie was joined in the shop by Jimmy Manley, who bought himself some sandwiches and invited himself to lunch, too, saying, "I was just on my way to see Mel and Alex with the autopsy report and a parcel of Cinzia's personal effects, which a motorcycle courier has just brought from Southampton."

So they were soon enjoying sandwiches, cold pork pies, Stilton and pickled onions, accompanied by small glasses of cool white wine. Jimmy said, "I won't spoil your lunch by reading out Dr Phipps' gory autopsy details, but, if you don't mind, I'll have a look at the parcel right away and see what we have. They couldn't find Cinzia's handbag, by the way – DC Drysdale confirmed she did have one with her when she bought her train ticket. The railway staff and the forensic people are looking for it, but either the murderer took it or it just got lost. This is a pity, because a lady's handbag quite often has many items of interest for we detectives! Let's see what we have here."

Jimmy tipped the contents of the parcel onto a sheet of newspaper. There was a small handkerchief, scented with what Melpomene recognized as Guerlain's 'Mitsouko', a pair of black leather gloves, a key-ring with two Yale keys, a packet of Sobranie Black Russian cigarettes containing six of the original ten, a matchbook labelled 'Davidoff of London', a twopenny bus ticket and a crumpled piece of paper. When Jimmy straightened this out, he said, "Now we have something very exciting! It appears to be a deposit slip headed 'Banca Popolare Di Palermo, 16 Threadneedle Street' for the not inconsiderable sum of £14,400, with the depositor's name listed as Sig.ra C Tagliamonte – my word! Somehow I don't think this represents Cinzia banking her tutor's stipend!"

"Will the bank give you any information about this?" asked Alex, "There are strict rules about privacy, aren't there?"

"There certainly are, as a rule!" said Jimmy, "I will have to see whether our friends in the Fraud Squad, particularly CI Patricia McMahon, have special dispensation to investigate accounts, or whether we will need to get an order from a judge. I'd dearly love to find out more about this transaction and any others she may have made!"

"I guess that those keys are to Cinzia's flat," said Melpomene, "now it's a murder investigation, will you need a search warrant, Jimmy?"

"Yes, but I've already put in for one. We were going to break in, but now we can do a search in a more civilized manner! Do you want to come with me, Mel? It's permissible, because after all, you are a Special Constable. I'll ring the station and get DC Drysdale to come too, since he's involved in the case, and then we can go, if you've finished lunch."

"One more cup of tea, please, and then I'm with you."

The Prestons' flat was in a mews, with garages below and outside stairs up to the flat entrances. They were about to go up to No. 4, when Jimmy said, "Hold on a moment, let's see whether one of these keys fits any of these garages."

He tried each key in a couple of doors and then said, "Ah hah!" as a key worked and he pulled a door open to disclose none other than a large green Armstrong Siddeley! He tried the driver's door, but it was locked, so he closed the garage door again and locked it.

"Later!" he said, "In any case we should let the forensics team have a go at it first. Up to the flat! Our surveillance people tell me that they have seen Cinzia go in and out recently, but that there has been no sign of Mervyn Preston since the incident at Liverpool Street station, so we needn't expect to find anyone in residence."

As Jimmy was opening the door, DC Drysdale arrived and was introduced to Melpomene, they shook hands and he said, "Dicky Drysdale, pleased to meet you. Oh, Jimmy, before I forget again, I've got something from that time at Paddington that I ought to pass on to you."

"OK, let's keep it for a few minutes, Dicky, but try not to forget it again – did you note it in your book?"

Inside the front door, they saw a few letters on the mat where they had been put through the slot. Dicky picked them up carefully by the corners and put them into a large envelope.

There was a short hallway, opening out to a sitting-room on the right and two bedrooms on the left, with single beds. "Looks as though it was a marriage in name only!" Melpomene remarked.

At the end of the hall was a kitchen with a big table, and through that a small bathroom and lavatory.

They went into the sitting-room which had a three-piece suite, quite new-looking, a coffee table, and a swivel chair in front of a roll-top bureau, with the top locked, as were the two drawers below.

Jimmy said, "Well, I won't force these locks, again I'll leave that for the forensic team – they probably have picks that will cope with these little locks."

Melpomene said, "Just a moment," and took a hair-pin out of her hair, "The hairdresser pinned up my curls while she was colouring them – I don't usually bother!"

She fiddled about with the pin in the lock of the roll top and than exclaimed, "Open Sesame!" and rolled it up, saying, "My Mama used to keep a jar of humbugs in her desk, and I found this trick out when I was about six!"

Inside the bureau was the usual arrangement of pigeon-holes and a rack of envelopes, with a blotter on the working surface, and hanging up on one side was a key.

"I'm feeling like Alice in Wonderland!" said Mel, and tried the key in the main drawers, one of which contained letters and the other a manila folder full of documents.

"We'll just take these to the station and look at them at leisure," said Jimmy, "What did you remember from Paddington, Dicky?"

"After I watched Cinzia pay for her ticket, a man with long black hair went to the window and asked whether the Southampton train stopped en route. He was told that there was only one stop, at Reading, so he said, "Give me a single to Reading, then.""

Chapter 34

"Did he and Cinzia speak to one another?" asked Jimmy.

"No, in fact she completely ignored him as she left the window, and he averted his face. I had the feeling that he knew her, though, but when she walked away he didn't follow her – there was still fifteen minutes to go before the train was due to leave. I watched to make sure that Cinzia got on board, but I didn't see what happened to the man."

"You say that he had long black hair, Dicky, how was he dressed?"

"Quite smartly, actually, in a nice suit and with polished shoes – like any respectable business man. He was tall and well-built."

Jimmy looked meaningfully at Mel and Alex, "Like the gunman who took out Serotti, perhaps! He could be what these gangs call an 'enforcer'! He was probably sorry he got rid of his Beretta and had to fall back on a small-calibre weapon this time!"

The doorbell rang and Dicky opened it and welcomed in two plain-clothes men carrying equipment cases.

Jimmy said, "Good, the scientific squad – come in and I'll show you what we have. I've already taken some documents from the desk, but we haven't been through any other drawers or cupboards – this is not a crime scene, but we're very interested in the former occupants. One of them won't be bothering you because she's in the morgue in Southampton, but her companion might possibly turn up. If he does, he should be detained! You know Dicky Drysdale, he will stay here with you if you have any questions. Good hunting!"

As Jimmy, Melpomene and Alex went down the steps, Mel said, "Did you forget to tell them about the Armstrong Siddeley, Jimmy, or do you want to leave that until later?"

Jimmy slapped his forehead, "Must be losing my grip! But actually, I've had another thought about that car. There's no record of either of the Prestons using it, but we were told it was registered to Osvaldo Scarletta through the Italian Embassy. That garage doesn't necessarily belong to Flat 4, even though

100

Cinzia was carrying a key to it. I think we should try to find out about the other occupants of these flats, but we need to be careful, we don't want to alert anyone prematurely, especially if we come across Signor Scarletta!"

"That sounds like a job for an experienced pretend estate agent!" said Melpomene, "Leave it to me, gentlemen! But first, my blood-tea levels are getting dangerously low – I think I saw a café in the street we turned out of, so will you join me?"

In the café, which failed to offer jam tarts but had an acceptable line of buttered scones and fairy cakes, they discussed tactics.

"Alex and I will wait in the car across the street, where there's a good view of the mews, in case of any drama. You can signal us if you need any help, Mel."

"And I've got my Beretta loaded and ready, Jimmy – but I promise not to use it unless I really have to!"

Melpomene put her glasses on and climbed the first set of outside stairs to Flat No. 1. This one had a bell-push with a label, 'Hargreaves', so she pressed it. Inside she heard some music stop – perhaps the occupant had switched off the wireless – and then the door opened and a woman in an apron appeared, with an enquiring expression on her face.

"Mrs Hargreaves?" said Mel, "Oh no dear, I'm jist the daily. Mr and Mrs Hargreaves are both orf. He works at the bank and he don't get back till late, most days. I think the Mrs 'as gorn to the West End, shopping. Dunno when she'll be back, sorry."

"What bank would that be?"

"Oh, I can never git the name right – it's one o' them furrin names, like Banko Popular or somethink."

"You've been very helpful – perhaps I'll call again later." The door was shut.

Mel gave a thumbs down signal in the direction of the car and went to the next flat, which was served by the same landing. There was no name by the bell-push, and pressing it brought no response, so she gave another thumbs down, trotted down and tried the next steps, which took her to Flat No. 3. This had a frame by the bell-push that had once held a label but was empty now – and pushing it was again fruitless, so Melpomene swore quietly under her breath and tried again at the set of steps after No. 4, where she could hear that the forensics team were still at work – moving furniture by the sound of it.

Flat No. 5 had flowerpots with geraniums on each side of the door, which had a cat-flap in it. Pushing the bell brought a young, quite pretty girl to the door, who said, straight away, blushing a little, "Oh, are you the lady from the council? I'm afraid that my husband isn't here, and I'm not sure I can help you – he looks after all the financial arrangements."

"No, I'm just making some enquiries," said Melpomene, "I'm Yvonne Herbison, from the estate agents, Ratcliffe and Hodges. You look as though you haven't been here long – perhaps you can tell me if any of your neighbours might be looking for a new place and thinking of moving out?"

"Would you like to come in – I'm Maureen Dodds – I mean Wilson, I'm not used to it yet! I was just going to have some tea, and it's so much nicer to have someone to chat with over a cup, if you've got the time – I haven't made any friends here yet."

"Why, I'd be glad to!" said Mel, "It'd be nice to sit down and rest my legs, I've been traipsing around the neighbourhood for ages!"

She was led into a sitting-room – the flat appeared to have a similar layout to No. 4 – and sat down while Mrs Wilson trotted off and soon came back with a tea-tray.

"You were quite right, Mrs Herbison, we haven't been here long – we come from Norfolk, and my husband has recently got a job at the Italian Embassy – we met at Norwich University, where we were both studying Modern European History – and as soon as he got the position here at the Embassy we decided not to wait any longer and so we got married!"

"So, how does he find diplomatic life, Mrs Wilson, or can I call you Maureen – and please call me Yvonne."

"It's all very strange – of course he's still in quite a junior position, under the Trade Attaché – but he's already finding his way around a bit. He tells me his colleagues are rather a mixed bunch – some are very helpful and some seem very suspicious and snap at him when he asks questions. Another member of the staff lives in the next flat here, and he won't even pass the time of day with me when I meet him in the mews – they have a little daughter, and when I tried to be pleasant with her, her mother called her indoors, quite sharply – I don't know why."

Chapter 35

Mel thought to herself, "I'd better make sure I don't run into the kid while I'm here – it could confuse Rosa to see her new teacher making house calls!"

To Maureen Wilson, she went on, "So are these flats owned by the Embassy? If they are, there is probably no point in my making enquiries about people moving out."

"Yes they are, Yvonne – we pay our rent monthly to the Comptroller's office. The furniture belongs to the Embassy as well, but we are allowed to bring in our own if we want. In fact, we have some of our wedding presents – crockery and linen mostly – stored in the garage waiting to be unpacked when we can get round to it."

"Don't you have a car, Maureen?"

"Not yet – we'll have to save up for one so we can do some touring when we take our annual holidays. For the moment we don't need one – it's only a short walk to the Embassy, and there are plenty of shops around here, and if I need to go to the West End there's always the tube. I think only a couple of these garages are used for cars – the Scarlettas next door – the ones with the small daughter – have a big saloon, and I saw a white Vauxhall drive in once, but it hasn't been around recently, as far as I've noticed."

"Well, thank you for the tea and the chat, Maureen, it's been very pleasant, but I ought to get on now. Are your next-door neighbours in at the moment, do you know?"

"No, I saw the mother and her little daughter leaving only an hour or so ago, and they were dressed neatly, as though they were going on a visit."

"Ah well – another time."

As Melpomene was making her way back to where the car was parked, she noticed that the front door of No. 4 stood open. Then DC Drysdale walked out onto the landing and waved to her.

"If you're going back to the car, Madam, would you ask DI Manley to come up, please – we've come across something that might interest him, as well as lifting a lot of prints."

As Mel reached the car, she saw that Alex and Jimmy were swivelled round facing one another on the front seat as much as they could, and playing chess on a pocket set. The van with the equipment was parked just behind their car.

"Sorry, but I'll have to interrupt your game – Jimmy is needed by the forensics boys!" she said, "Who was winning, anyway?"

She sat down in the back seat, and Alex said, "It was anyone's game at this stage, actually – neither of us would qualify as Grand Masters, I'm afraid! How did you get on with your enquiries?"

Mel told him about her conversations and said, "I'll tell Jimmy it might be a good opportunity for his men to have a look at that Armstrong Siddeley – I was informed by Mrs Wilson that the Scarlettas are elsewhere for a while today. She and her husband could be useful contacts – he has only been at the Embassy a short while, so he's unlikely to have been corrupted yet, and she's very pleasant and intelligent. I think I'll go up and see what they've found that they're so keen for Jimmy to see."

"I'll come too, Mel, I'm getting fed up with sitting here, chess or no chess!"

They walked into the sitting-room to find Jimmy putting some white gloves on and opening a big buff envelope.

"This was hidden – but we're well aware of most of the cunning places that crims use that they think are secure. This envelope, for example, was taped to the underside of one of the bureau drawers. It'll be checked for prints, of course, but I'm being careful and using these cotton gloves so as not to smudge them. Now let's see what's in it!"

He slid the contents out onto the bureau. There were several sheets of paper, one of which looked like a bank statement and others that were typewritten letters on headed paper, and a small notebook or diary.

"I can cope with the bank statement," said Jimmy, "but I'm afraid my Italian is not up to making any sense of the correspondence, so we'll pass these over to Hortense – she's fluent in the language. If this statement refers to Cinzia's account, she was a very wealthy woman! But somehow I reckon she was just handling the funds for someone else."

"What's in the book – is it in Italian too?" asked Melpomene.

"Hard to tell – it seems to be in some sort of code – nothing but groups of four letters or numbers. We shall have to hand it over to a cryptographer – I wonder whether Adrian Fitz-Hugh has any experts in cyphers on his staff?"

Jimmy slid the letters and book back into the envelope and put that into a file wallet before he went on, "We'll get these checked for fingerprints before we pass them on, and our typewriter expert may be able to tell us what sort of machine the typing was done on – I believe that the fonts vary from company to company and country to country. Did you notice that there were accents over some of the letters? – You don't get those on an English machine. I know that French uses accents, but I don't know about Italian."

He turned to the forensics people. "When you've finished up here, have a look in the garage and see whether you can open the doors of the Armstrong Siddeley without doing any damage or leaving any marks – I don't want the owner to know we've been having a poke round. You could see if you can lift any prints from the obvious places, like door handles, though. Give the keys to Dicky Drysdale when you've done with them – can you give him a lift back to Mile End Road? I'm going back to Mr and Mrs Crabbe's agency with them."

Back at the office, Melpomene said, "Who's for a cup of tea? I had one with Maureen Wilson, but that seems ages ago! Any telephone calls while we were out, Marjorie and Winnie?"

"Yes, your Mama rang, Mel – nothing urgent, she just wanted to know how things were with you in general. Shall I get her for you?"

Melpomene simply chatted with her Mama about inconsequential things, then remembered something.

"Have you read in the papers about a mysterious death on the Paddington to Southampton train? Well, she was a person involved in our current case – you may or may not be amused to know that her name is – was – Cinzia, which is, of course, the Italian spelling of your own name, Cynthia. I hope this doesn't upset you, Mama!"

"Don't distress yourself, my dear! I am not in the least superstitious, and I already know someone of that name here in Woodhampton – she has a nice little hat shop! But be careful!"

Chapter 36

The telephone rang again – Alex answered, and found that it was Jimmy once more, saying, "I remembered that DC Arturo Bellini, at Shepherds Bush, helped us out with Italian translation before, when we were interviewing Angelo Serotti, so I asked him to come to Mile End Road and have a look at those letters that were hidden in the flat. He had no difficulty working out that they were from various banks in Italy, addressed to Signora Tagliamonte, confirming arrangements for transfers of money from Banca Popolare Di Palermo to her deposit accounts. They also each said, one way or another, that the necessary account numbers and codes would be sent under separate cover, by registered post. We haven't come across any such letters – those that were on the doormat at the flat were ordinary post, not registered – and the dates on the transfer arrangements were four to six weeks ago, so it seems that Cinzia must have put them away somewhere."

"Maybe," suggested Alex, "she put them with the other codified stuff in that little notebook – it would be hard to know quite what is in there, and Cinzia is certainly not going to say now. Perhaps if we ever get our hands on Mervyn Preston he might be able to enlighten us. If there's nothing else, Jimmy, we'll be heading home now – we'll see you tomorrow, will we? We'd be very interested to know about fingerprints, and any other forensic evidence that's come up."

Alex rang off and turned to Mel, "I forgot to ask him whether he found someone to look at that code notebook – I suppose there's no real rush – let's call it a day now and go and have a nice meal and a relaxing evening."

"Before you go," said Marjorie, "we had a rather plaintive call from Philomena Hotchkiss this afternoon. She wasn't asking you to ring back – she said she didn't want to interrupt whatever you were doing – but she and Eric had rather lost track of their case and wondered whether you could find an opportunity to fill them in, some time. I took it upon myself to tell her one or two things, like the story of Cinzia – she and Eric had already been informed about Angelo Serrotti's shooting, of course, and everyone at Perrin and Wesley knew about the arrest of Ronald Sedgwick, too."

"Oh – mea culpa, mea maxima culpa!" said Melpomene, "I've been terribly remiss – after all, she and Eric are our primary clients – I'll telephone them this evening from home."

Mrs Mountain had performed up to her usual standard, and Mel and Alex enjoyed a meal that Mrs M referred to as "parsnip and celery soup, follered by gormay toad in the 'ole".

Then, before they settled to perusing the newspapers or solving the day's cryptic crossword respectively, Melpomene asked, "Alex, have you got the Hotchkiss' number in your little book?"

When Philomena answered, Melpomene apologized profusely for their neglect and then had a thought, "If you and Eric have eaten and aren't doing anything in particular tonight, would you like to come round here and we'll have a glass or two of wine and a nice chat, as well as bringing you up to date? – Oh good – you know where our flat is, we're only fifteen minutes away from you by car. See you soon!"

Mel had only solved a few clues when the doorbell rang and she went to welcome Phil and Eric.

"We just parked in the street," said Eric, "I hope that's all right – there didn't seem to be any signs."

"That's fine – we sometimes park there ourselves." said Melpomene, "Please come into the sitting-room and make yourselves comfortable. What can I offer you – we have a choice of sherries, or French or Italian vermouths, and Alex has a single-malt scotch he seems to like quite a lot! I'm more of a wine person."

"What a nice room!" exclaimed Phil, "I love the Art Deco sofa! May I sit on it, please? We've got rather boring stuff at home!"

Once everyone was settled with a glass of their choice, Eric asked, "We assume that you two had a hand in the arrest of Ronald Sedgwick, for which I'm extremely grateful! Apart from the annoying ways in which he was harassing me, he could easily have tricked me into a criminal conspiracy from which I might have had extreme difficulty in extricating myself! Have you had any success in tracking down Osvaldo, my other bête noir?"

"We appreciate your gratitude," said Alex, "but we were not directly involved – we simply suggested that the Fraud Squad might find something interesting at Perrin and Wesley. They and other branches of the police have their eyes on others around the firm, too, but we shouldn't talk about them yet."

"As for friend Osvaldo," said Mel, "we've found out more about him, and I think our friend, Detective-Inspector Jimmy Manley, might be able to pounce on him when the time is right, but meanwhile we are all more interested in keeping him under observation, hoping that he will lead us to others involved in what is beginning to look like a large-scale scheme for concealing illicit money transfers between England and various continental countries. It's something of a pity that Cinzia Preston, née Tagliamonte, wasn't picked up earlier, which might have saved her from being assassinated, which we suspect was meant to shut her up!"

Alex took over, "Some of us have come to the conclusion that the killings of Cinzia and Angelo Serotti were carried out by the same person, but this is by no means certain. We have a name, which I prefer not to mention at the moment, but we have no clear idea where he might be lurking."

Eric asked, "I remember you were asking me once if I had any dealings with a firm called Castelbianco – do you suspect that it is playing some part in all this skullduggery?"

"At least indirectly, yes," replied Alex, "we have been told that Osvaldo works there, under an assumed surname. He is known at the Italian embassy – which we have no reason to believe is aware of his criminal connections – as Osvaldo Scarletta, and at Castelbianco and elsewhere as Osvaldo Griguolo. Our contacts at the Sûreté have a thick dossier on him – he is known to have contacts with the Italian mafia and also to have had dealings with a bank in Lyons which is suspected of facilitating illegal international money transfers, so it is quite likely that Castelbianco, in conjunction with Banca Popolare di Palermo, which conveniently occupies the ground floor of its building in Threadneedle Street, is a link in the corrupt money pipeline."

"I don't know about anyone else," said Philomena, who had been listening enthralled, "but I'll need some time to absorb all this – and I'd like to suggest we switch topics, if you don't mind, otherwise I'll be dreaming about it all night!"

"Quite right, Phil!" said Melpomene, "and we could have some hot chocolate while we do that. Have you seen anything good at the pictures lately? – we've hardly had the time for it ourselves, which is a pity!"

Chapter 37

"Since you ask," replied Philomena, "we went a couple of days ago to the Capitol Cinema in the Haymarket to see a thriller by that new English director, Alfred Hitchcock. It's called 'The Lodger: A Story of the London Fog' and we enjoyed it very much, although it's a silent movie. Apparently Hitchcock is from the East End, so the settings are really authentic. I think it would appeal to you two, as it's about crime and detection! But," she went on, "Melpomene should take care – the killer in that story was choosing ladies with blonde curls as his victims!"

"Maybe we'll go and pick up some hints!" said Mel, "Now, who would like hot chocolate? We have Horlicks, too, but not everyone fancies the taste of malted milk."

"Well, I do!" said Eric, "if it's good enough for Arctic explorers it's good enough for me! But while we're having our warm drinks, I should remember to tell you about some recent events of interest at Perrin and Wesley. Of course, the arrest of Ronald Sedgwick caused a major commotion, and people were looking askance at their colleagues for a day or two, wondering who else had been complicit. But what I thought was significant, was that there were at least two people who seemed over-anxious to declare publicly that they had been suspicious of Sedgwick for a long time. One of these was that woman who got off on the wrong foot talking to Philomena at a social event once – Sylvia Myers – she's in charge of a special section which deals with firms in the Far East, so she has a lot to do with foreign currencies, and she went around saying that she had developed doubts about Sedgwick's handling of overseas investors."

"Yes!" said Philomena, "I wouldn't trust her any further than I could throw her! And you told me about this naval type, Commodore Lane, too, Eric – what was it you said about him?"

"Yes, he claimed he'd never trusted Sedgwick, but he was certainly very chummy with him – only the day before the police came for him, the two of them rolled into work after a late lunch, looking a bit the worse for wear, and Lane had his arm round Sedgwick's shoulders in a very friendly way! But we've slipped back into talking shop, so let's leave this subject before we give Phil nightmares again! What leisure activities do you go in for, Mel and Alex? I know that Alex is a golfer like me – we must make a date for a round at a local club some day, but I believe Mel is no keener on golf than Phil, so they'll have to make their own arrangements if they want to do something together."

Melpomene rose to the bait, "I've always found that a day spent in the haute couture establishments of Bond Street can be very entertaining and worthwhile – how about joining me one day, Phil? Fenwick's is a favourite of mine – I particularly like its restaurant, as well as the fashion departments."

The time slipped by comfortably as they chatted on, until Eric looked at his watch and said, "Some people have to go to work in the morning – thanks for a lovely evening – we shall have to return the favour before long!"

After they'd made their goodbyes to the others. Alex said, "I must make myself a note to look up Commodore Lane on the Navy List – I intended to do this before, but then it slipped my memory. We could make enquiries about Sylvia Myers while we're about it, too. Have you heard about your tutoring job yet, Mel? It would be good to see whether there are any associates of Scarletta that need to be looked at. Oh, dear – I think Philomena was right – we shouldn't be worrying about all this just before bedtime!"

As soon as they reached the office the next morning, Alex telephoned Jimmy at Mile End Road to ask him what the forensics team had garnered from the Prestons' flat.

"You already know about the bank documents – we've got some of our financial experts tracking the transactions down – even without the codes, the Fraud Squad and their continental colleagues are able to get most of the information. We'll get a comprehensive report in a week or two, they tell me."

"What about the book with the codes, Jimmy?" asked Alex.

"Ah, now that's rather interesting – Adrian Fitz-Hugh has an old wartime comrade from the DMI, the Directorate of Military Intelligence, who worked on the codes used by spies, during and after the War, in a Section called MI1: Codes and Cyphers. The War Office still maintains a small staff for this purpose – even in peacetime, foreign countries still need watching! So he's passed them Cinzia's little book to have a look at. No news yet, I'm afraid!"

"Any interesting fingerprints?"

"Not really, the prints in the Prestons' flat and on the envelope taped to the drawer were, those that could be seen clearly, mostly Cinzia's and her common-law husband's, of course, with a few corresponding to those on the gun that Preston passed to the mystery woman. This brings me to the Armstrong Siddeley car. As I instructed them, the forensics people didn't try to open the car, but they found plenty of good prints on the door handles and windows. There was a lovely complete print of a left hand on the windscreen – this looked as though whoever had wiped down the windscreen had steadied himself while he stretched across. Interestingly, this was found to belong to whoever used the Beretta to dispatch Serotti and his driver, that is, Gian Carlo Passarella, whose prints were sent to us by Hortense Deslarges at the Sûreté."

"This is all very satisfactory, Jimmy," said Alex, "We shall have to be patient, but the jigsaw puzzle seems to be building up!"

Melpomene had been following all this on the extension ear-piece, congratulated Jimmy and went on, "We've been thinking we ought to direct our attention now to Perrin and Wesley and Castelbianco. We had Eric and Philomena Hotchkiss round at our place last night, and it looks as though we could have profitable conversations with several of the staff at P and W – don't know so much about Castelbianco. And Marjorie has just told me that I've now had my tutoring job at the Italian Embassy confirmed, so that might be another useful avenue. I shall have to be very careful if and when I talk to Scarletta, and as I have said before, I have no intention of pumping his little daughter! Of course, we'll keep you informed all the time – we'll see you later!"

Alex said, "Winnie, could you find out who we should approach about consulting the Navy List, and where? I've never had occasion to do that, but the War Office might be a good starting point."

"Or we could try Adrian Fitz-Hugh," suggested Winnie, "leave it to me – I suppose you want to check on the *bona fides* of Commodore Lane, is that right?"

"As usual, Winnie, you are right on the case! And I don't know where we would find out whether he has ever blotted his copybook apart from that affray in the pub that Patricia McMahon put us on to – he wasn't convicted on that occasion."

Chapter 38

Alex asked, "So when do you go and tutor the kids in English, Mel – has this been all arranged?"

"No, the message that Marjorie took was that I should telephone Mrs Abbott at the embassy and discuss arrangements with her. I'll try her now – can you get me Mrs Abbott, please, Marjorie?"

"Hello, Mrs Abbott, Henrietta Musgrave here. Thanks for letting me know that the tutoring job has been approved. Now, when should I come to the Embassy to start the lessons? And, if possible, I'd like to meet the parents at some stage – they might want to satisfy themselves that I'm a suitable person! – right, ten o'clock tomorrow it is then – I look forward to seeing you and the children again!"

Melpomene rang off and let the others know, "It sounds as though I'll be going there on Tuesdays and Thursdays, from 10 until noon. Mrs Abbott says that's what the children were used to with Mrs Preston, but it can be changed later if necessary."

"Or when you get found out!" said Alex, "When are you going to meet the parents?"

"Mrs Abbott will arrange that later, she says. Meanwhile, Marjorie or Winnie, can you telephone Lucy Stafford, my hairdresser, and make an appointment for me, please – I'd like to freshen up the auburn in my hair – it's not a permanent colour, so it comes out a bit every time I wash it. And on the way back I'll call into the newsagents to pick up some reading materials for the children – I decided I'd get some comics to lighten up their studies a bit. I thought of the Rupert Bear strip they have every day in the Daily Express – I used to devour these stories when I was younger – they have little verses with the pictures as well as short prose paragraphs, so they could be good reading exercises for the class, whatever their ages."

A few minutes later, Winnie hung up the telephone and said "Lucy says she can fit you in if you turn up at the salon in an hour – I said it was just for colouring – that was right, Mel, wasn't it?"

"Good, thanks Winnie. Now should I get everybody something for lunch on the way back – I shall be passing that nice new delicatessen shop. I fancy some sort of salami or chorizo myself, with some potato salad and some nice bread or panini – how about you, Alex?"

"Sounds fine, Mel, just get something that you know I like – you could add some pickles, too. Winnie, what would you like Melpomene to get for you? I know Marjorie always brings a lunch packed by her Mum."

"But maybe I'll sample some of your stuff too!" said Marjorie, "You wouldn't want me to stick to my fish-paste and cucumber sandwiches alone, would you?"

When Melpomene returned after a couple of hours, with an audacious hair colour and wearing some very serious-looking black-rimmed glasses, everyone fell ravenously upon the lunch items she had brought and nothing much was said for a while.

Finally, Winnie sat back and announced, "You had a call while you were out, Melpomene, something you've been waiting for, from Thelma Harris, Sir Adrian's personal assistant. Alex listened in and I took shorthand notes – I'll type them up in a moment, but the gist is that the whereabouts of Gian Carlo Passarella are now known. Patricia McMahon's people have located him in a seaside boarding-house in Brighton, where he is known as Charlie Parsons, poses as a commercial traveller in industrial paints and is a regular caller to many small factories along the south coast."

Melpomene clapped her hands and said, "Wonderful – did Thelma say he would be picked up?"

"No – I gather that the idea is that they will keep him under close observation, in the hope that some other members of the organization can be swept up as well. I'll give you my transcript of the whole conversation in a little while, Mel."

Later on in the afternoon, there was another welcome piece of news – this time DI Jimmy Manley rang to say that the elusive Mr Preston had tried to sneak back into his flat late last night, not realising that it was under surveillance, and had been nabbed and taken to Mile End Road station for questioning!

He went on to tell Melpomene, "He has been pretty close-lipped so far, but I intend to confront him with the mysterious woman he passed the gun to, with the hope that one or other of them will be provoked into giving us some useful information. I'm seeking permission for this from the courts, as she has been held in a remand centre prior to being interrogated and charged – so far she has been singularly uncommunicative, and our continental colleagues have not yet found a match for her fingerprints in any of their systems, neither in France nor in Italy. We are holding her on a charge of possession of an unlicensed fire-arm, but this can't be extended indefinitely and she will have to face a court or be released. Have you been told about Passarella?"

"Yes, by Patricia McMahon – she says he's using the cover as a paint sales representative, which makes me think that, as we surmised for Stratton and Son, these crooks are using small industrial firms as fronts for their drug smuggling and gun-running activities. By the way, Jimmy, tomorrow I'm going to give my first English lesson to the Italian kids at the embassy, so that'll be interesting! I'll let you know how I get on, of course. Another thought – when your people were picking up Preston, did any of the other residents of the flats observe this? I would prefer that the Scarletta family, especially, did not get wind of anything that might put them on their guard."

"You can rest assured on that, Mel, it was Cec in charge of the arrest team, and he knows to be particularly careful. Have fun at the embassy and we'll share our experiences later!"

"This all seems to be proceeding well," said Alex, "our next phase is to find out more about the goings-on at Perrin and Wesley and Castelbianco. I thought I might ring Eric Hotchkiss this evening and see whether it would make sense for me to visit him at work – I wondered whether he could introduce me to his trusted friends and perhaps point out the people he regards as dubious, including Sylvia Myers and the shady Commodore Lane. Earlier, I tried to see whether the custodians of the Navy List were prepared to answer leading questions from a member of the public, but I was told that they were only permitted to deal with Naval officers or through official channels, so I shall have to see what Adrian can do."

"Well, my love," said Melpomene, "it looks as though we might each have a full day tomorrow – let's go home and we can think about our plans after dinner. Marjorie and Winnie – I shan't be in first thing tomorrow, but Alex will – won't you dear? I shall be wending my way to the embassy by tube, dressed in my best schoolmarm outfit and carrying a briefcase full of highly educational materials, such as comic strips from the pages of the Daily Express. See you all later, I'll relate my experiences!"

Chapter 39

As he had decided, after dinner Alex telephoned Eric Hotchkiss and between the two of them worked out a plan of campaign for his visit to Perrin and Wesley the next day, while Melpomene made some notes about her teaching session at the embassy, including cutting out the Rupert Bear adventures from the Daily Express. Once they had settled on their respective programmes, they relaxed, Mel with a crossword – she had glanced at the ones in the Express, but had turned up her nose and returned to the one in The Times – while Alex was catching up on his favourite reading of detective novels. At the moment he was enjoying a change from Agatha Christie, turning instead to 'Whose Body?' by Dorothy L. Sayers, a writer he had just encountered, with her new character, Lord Peter Wimsey.

He was obviously entranced, because when Melpomene announced she was off for her bath and bed, he merely grunted without looking up.

At five to ten the next morning, Melpomene walked into the foyer of the Italian Embassy and went up to the reception desk. The man said, "Ah yes, Madam – Mrs Musgrave, isn't it? I remember you from the other day. Mrs Abbott said you would be coming this morning, so I have prepared a badge for you to wear, so that you won't be constantly asked to state your business – we have to be careful here, of course. I'll ring for someone to take you to the children's classroom – I understand you've already been introduced to your students. Mrs Abbott will catch up with you later, but she has been called away to deal with an administrative matter that will occupy her for an hour or so – she asked me to give you her apologies."

When she walked into the students' room – it was not only a classroom, but also their common-room, Mel thought – the five students stood up, but didn't say anything, so Mel said, "Good morning children, it would be nice if you were to greet me when I arrive. You could say, 'Good morning, Mrs Musgrave', but maybe some of you know other English greetings. How about you, Rosa – have I got your name right? – what else could you say? Don't be scared – I don't bite!"

Rosa Scarletta said, in a small voice, "Pleased to meet you, teacher!"

Melpomene congratulated her, and the ice now seemed generally broken, so that the others tried their greetings, too.

After that, Mel asked who was prepared to talk about themself, as she had asked when she met them first, and, one by one, at various levels of fluency, four of the five managed to deliver their speeches. The oldest girl, Beatrice Manfredi, whose English was the best of the group, explained that this was because she had been attending the American school in Rome for nearly two years, so Melpomene asked her if she would be happy to help the smallest boy, Gerardo Ferrero, who had been reluctant to speak, saying to her, "Please explain to him, in Italian, that he shouldn't be ashamed. You could tell him that Mrs Musgrave knows very little Italian except the names of some foods and wines!"

From that point on, Mel thought that the lesson proceeded very well, and she decided to keep Rupert Bear in reserve for a later meeting. The finishing time of twelve o'clock seemed to come round very quickly, and as Mel gathered up some written work to take home and correct, she said "Goodbye, class, until Thursday when I'll see you again – you are all doing beautifully! Arrivederci a tutti!"

Mrs Abbott had been waiting at the back of the room, and as they left together, said, "That looked as though it went off very well, Mrs Musgrave! Would you be prepared to have a word with two of the parents now? I spoke to Signor Ponzi and Signor Scarletta, and they were happy to meet you for a few minutes – I'll take you to the cafeteria to see them. Would you like to have something to eat and then you could chat at the table – they only serve light dishes at lunchtime here, so that some work will get done in the afternoons! I'm sorry I couldn't be there at the beginning of the class, but I was called to a meeting of all the middle-level managers. I can't divulge the subject of the meeting, except to say that it was also attended by some very senior members of the English Foreign Office and a high-ranking Metropolitan Police officer. Ah, here we are – this is our little lunch-room – the attachés and higher-ups have a much more elaborate place up on the top floor where a lot of diplomacy goes on over the gourmet meals and champagne."

Mrs Abbott showed Mel how to order at the counter from the items displayed. She chose a ham and cheese panino and a fruit salad, and was shown to a table where two men were eating and chatting. Mrs Abbot made the introductions and left, and the two stood up, shook hands and invited Mel to a spare chair.

Signor Scarletta turned out to be very different from the mental image that Melpomene had been building up – he was tall, with an athletic build, blue eyes and light brown hair, while his companion, Ponzi, was what Mel would have described as typically Italian, with slicked down black hair, slightly portly and not very tall.

"And how did you find your pupils, Signora Musgrave?" asked Scarletta, "I shall, of course, ask my Rosa what she thought of you! I must say that she was not terribly fond of Signora Preston, so I was not sorry when we were told she had left, under mysterious circumstances!"

"Not so very mysterious, Osvaldo!" said Ponzi, "Unless you are referring to the reason for her murder – it has become clear that the woman reported in the newspapers to have been found shot on the Southampton train was Signora Cinzia Preston!"

"I beleve that Rosa is going to do quite well," said Melpomene, "and so is your daughter Gabriela, Signor Ponzi. The younger of the boys will need some extra attention, but I have no doubt that we can bring them all up to an acceptable standard of conversational English by, say, mid-year. I have plans for their written work, also, but this will take more time."

"How are you enjoying your lunch, Signora?" said Ponzi, "This cafeteria is quite pleasant, is it not? We, as attachés, are entitled to use the more elaborate facilities on a higher floor, but I for one would rather have a more modest lunch here – upstairs we are too easily involved in other people's concerns and this can be very time-consuming. Last Friday my friend Osvaldo here was away from the embassy, so I went to lunch up there and soon found myself in the middle of a dispute which concerned serious accusations brought by outside bodies – there was a follow-up meeting called this morning that wasted another couple of hours and had nothing to do with my section at all – our responsibility is liaison with your Board of Trade over matters of licencing and patents, and nothing of that sort came up either yesterday or this morning. "

Chapter 40

"Now, now, Fabio," interjected Scarletta, "we should not burden Signora Musgrave with our obsessions – she is here to educate our children, not to concern herself with our troubles! How long have you been teaching like this, Signora?"

Melpomene was glad of the chance to strengthen her assumed role, so said, "Not very long at all – since I graduated in Social Anthropology I have mainly been doing research into oral communication, so this practical work has been valuable to me in putting theory into practice. I shall, for example, watch the relationships that develop in my little group with great interest. No doubt this embassy as a whole would offer me a far more complex web of interactions, but I shall hardly have the opportunity to follow them up to any great extent."

"Maybe the chance will arise," said Signor Ponzi, "but, for the moment, Osvaldo and I must return to our tiresome meeting. It has been a pleasure talking to you, Signora. Maybe we can do this again in a while – Gabriela tells me you will be back here on Thursday for the next lesson. Oh, I have just spotted a colleague of ours to whom I would like to introduce you, if you would permit me. Her name is Signorina Primavera Guzzi, and she is a journalist working for the Press Attaché here."

He led Melpomene over to a table occupied by only one woman – a smartly turned-out blonde who was sipping at a glass while a waitress cleared away her lunch things.

"Primavera, my dear," said Ponzi, "may I introduce Signora Musgrave – I'm afraid I don't know your first name – our new English tutor for the embassy children, who has started only this morning. Maybe you will be better able than Osvaldo and I to describe to her all the complex relationships among our staff here!"

Melpomene almost forgot to introduce herself as Henrietta, but managed it without stumbling. Signorina Guzzi smiled and asked her to join her, saying, "I'm finishing off my lunch with a glass of the house Pinot Grigio – the embassy, of course, insists on serving only Italian wines, though I believe it has been known for champagnes to be served at special functions – so can I order a glass for you, Signora?"

"That would be very nice – and please call me Henrietta! Have you worked here at the embassy for very long? I started only this morning, so I know very little about it and the people here. I am principally a social anthropologist, rather than a teacher, so I am very interested in the dynamics of complex organisations."

"I have been working here just over a year," said Primavera, "I came here straight from Verona, where I was an editor on Italy's first monthly women's magazine, 'La Donna'. I came here because I broke up with my *fidanzato*, my fiancé, who is a photographer on the magazine – I'm sorry to burden you with my troubles, but I haven't yet got over it completely – and I find that there are no women here in the embassy who are at all *sympatico*! You will quickly find out, from your professional viewpoint, that many of the people in an embassy such as this behave as though it were a nest of snakes! Oh, I am carrying on rather, please excuse me!"

Mel asked, "Did you have much to do with Cinzia Preston? I gather that she was not generally liked – I hope that her reputation has not been transferred to me simply because I inherited her job. What was it about her that people objected to?"

"Well, I can tell you it was not so much criticism of her teaching, or of her behaviour toward the children, but rather that she seemed to be overly inquisitive about the officers of the embassy and their work. She would button-hole individuals, here in the cafeteria, or in the lounges or meeting-rooms, and ask searching questions to the point of annoyance – there is a general culture of discretion here, arising out of the sensitive nature of much of the transactions with outside bodies, so her approach tended to grate! She was inclined to ignore evasive signals and ride rough-shod over them, even when her target resorted almost to rudeness to get rid of her! I can tell you that when the news trickled through that she was dead, more than one person here was heard to express somewhat vindictive satisfaction! But I can't think that it was anyone in the embassy who lost patience to the extent of bumping her off!"

"Well, I will take that as a warning, Primavera – I hope you didn't mind me saying that I'm professionally interested in seeing how the place operates. I shall try not to risk turning anyone off with my naïve enquiries! Perhaps you could let me know if there is anybody in particular I should avoid. I expect to be teaching here for some months, so I'm in no rush to build up a picture of the social organization of this place."

Primavera decided that it was time for her to return to her duties, saying, "I'm working on a new series of articles on Italian fashion trends for the Woman's Weekly – His Excellency is keen to promote cultural exchange between our two countries, and he thinks that up to now the French have had an unfair edge, so my series might help – and I might even get some new outfits myself!"

Melpomene said, "It's been lovely talking to you, Primavera, you must keep me in touch with your work – it might freshen up my wardrobe thinking! Will you be here on Thursday for another talk over lunch?"

"Certainly, and if we're to be friends, please call me Vera!"

"So you must call me Hettie, then – but please, not Henry or Hen!"

When she got back to the office, Melpomene found that Alex was still out, and asked Marjorie and Winnie whether they had heard from him.

"Not so far," replied Winnie, "and how did you get on with your little pupils?"

"Quite well," she replied, "but I'll save up my story until Alex is back – there was more to my visit than just the English lesson! I may have made a very useful contact, as well as talking to Signor Scarletta and his colleague. Any interesting letters or telephone calls?"

"Nothing of any value in the post," said Marjorie, "but there were two telephone calls that could be promising when they are followed up. Archie Staples said he had some useful information for us, but he preferred to wait until he could talk to you or Alex. The other call was from your Mama – she said she wasn't complaining, but you haven't spoken to her for a while, since you told her about Cinzia!"

"She's quite right, of course – please get her for me and I'll try to put her mind at rest that there have been no further murders, kidnappings, parcel bombs or anonymous letters – I assume that there haven't been any such excitements while I was out of the office?"

Chapter 41

Lady Cynthia's secretary, Mavis, answered the call, telling Melpomene that she had just missed her mother, "She has gone into Woodhampton to do some shopping. Shall I say you called and get her to ring back when she returns, or will you try again? She will certainly be in this evening, because she and Lady Isabel are entertaining a few friends for dinner."

"Oh, I'll ring this evening – unless the guests are too important to be disturbed!"

"I don't think so, they are Major and Mrs Buckmaster and their daughter Phoebe, and Superintendent Wilkinson and his wife – they would probably be happy to hear from you, anyway."

"Oh good – I can kill a flock of birds with one stone! Thanks, Mavis."

To Marjorie and Winnie she said that she had a busy day and was ready to go home, so would catch up with Alex later.

As it happened, he arrived at the flat only a few minutes after Mel, looking rather distraught, saying, "What a day – I'm ready for a drink now!" and pouring himself a large Scotch.

"If you're willing to tell me what happened," said Melpomene, "I'll get a glass of wine and join you in the sitting room, and you can tell me all about it. Were you unmasked by the opposition, or what?"

"Fortunately, not! My cover as Eric's old school friend is still intact – I'm contemplating switching careers from life insurance to stockbroking, and finding out what's involved in the move, not necessarily to Perrin and Wesley, but to a similarly reputable firm."

"Said he, with his tongue in his cheek!" muttered Mel.

"It turned out to be a promising subterfuge," said Alex, "a lot of these types have convinced themselves that they are experts, and are only too happy to take a beginner under their wings – making sure, of course, that they don't actually divulge any useful inside information! No, the problem today is that I was buttonholed by one after another, all telling me how I should approach it – and every one different! My head is spinning with it all – and of course, what I was really listening out for were clues to possible dishonest behaviour."

"So who did you talk to? I assume you started with some of Eric's colleagues who he believes are honest?"

"That's right. I was introduced first to Frank Collins – he's a reliable fellow, one of Eric's old friends. He works on what they call 'the Cairo desk', which I'm informed is shorthand for any dealings beyond Italy – not including India and China, which are handled by a specialist group. From what he told me, I don't believe that the likelihood of shenanigans there is worth considering. The Far East is a different matter, the Japanese Yakuza and the Chinese Tongs are known to be very active in gunrunning and drugs, principally opium, so they have their own systems for money dealings, but these are not handled in London but in places like Singapore and Hong Kong. Frank seems fairly confident that we needn't bother to investigate anything to the east of Italy."

"It sounds as though you have taken Frank into your confidence – was that safe?"

"Eric thinks so, he has great faith in him, as he's known him for years. So Frank knows that I'm a sleuth – but I haven't told him about you, just in case! The next question I asked him was about Ronald Sedgwick's associates – just because he's been taken out of circulation doesn't mean that other rotten apples are not still lurking in the barrel. I'll have to look again at the notes I made on the information that Patricia McMahon gave us – the others who were questioned at the time were Sir William Carr-Hazelton, Commodore Gordon Lane and Wilson Tuckett. But the only one who was taken into custody and charged was Sedgwick."

"So was Mr Collins able to tell you anything useful about these people, or even suggest any others that deserve scrutiny?"

"Not really, Mel – but I'll certainly go to him when I have specific questions. The other avenue that I've been pursuing today is simply trying to paint myself a picture of how the various parts of the company fit together – this is something that you've taught me, from your viewpoint as a social anthropologist – and I'm coming to the conclusion that it is relationships that will give us the real clues here – wheels within wheels, as they say! But enough of me, Mel – how did you get on at the Italian embassy?"

"It was very pleasant, I must say, Alex! I find that I quite enjoy teaching – the kids are very polite and help each other, too. They range in English ability from one little boy who can hardly say a word to a girl who is quite fluent, having been attending an American school in Rome. But after the class I met two of the parents over a light lunch, including the notorious Osvaldo Scarletta, who turns out to be a very charming man! Of course, I confined myself to safe topics of conversation, but I think that the cordial relationship we established will be valuable on a later occasion when I might want to tackle more sensitive matters. And he and his friend, Fabio Ponzi, introduced me to a woman who I intend really to cultivate – she is a journalist who has been at the embassy long enough to build a picture, but not so long as to become an established part of the environment. She is called Primavera Guzzi, and we are already on such terms as to be using short forms of our names – Vera and Hettie! I remembered in time that my name is Henrietta – it would be only too easy to make a slip with it!"

"So, why do you think she will be particularly useful, Hettie – I mean Mel! – because she is a woman, or what?"

"Mainly because she is a journalist, working under the Press Attaché, so that her colleagues will not expect her to keep her lip buttoned like other people in the embassy, who have adopted a very correct, even formal, attitude because of the need for diplomatic discretion. By the way, she is writing a series on Italian fashion trends for the Woman's Weekly, which I shall keep an eye on!"

"Did you get anything useful from Primavera today, or are you just banking on her as a potential source?"

"She told me a lot about Cinzia Preston, Alex. Apparently she made herself unpopular by being too keen to ask questions, so I take that as a word to the wise – I shall have to be more subtle! Now I want to telephone Mama – she's entertaining the Buckmasters and the Wilkinsons to dinner, so we might get a chance to have a word or two with them while we're at it. I don't know why Mama called me at work while I was out today, so that's the first order of business – and I mustn't interrupt their eating too much, so let me see what stage they've reached. Excuse me Alex, I'll use the telephone in the hall – perhaps we ought to get an extension in the sitting-room here, so we don't have to stand in the draught."

Chapter 42

"Hello, Mama, it's Mel – did you want to tell me something when you rang before? If you were simply making sure we're both all right, you can rest assured – our case is proceeding nicely and there have been no nasty moments recently."

"No, no, Melpomene, my darling – I have resolved not to fret about you and that seems to be working! This morning I wanted to pass on a piece of news David Wilkinson told me about. But since we have David and Gillian here for dinner – we haven't gone in to the table yet – he can tell you himself, so I'll call him to the telephone."

"Hello, Melpomene, nice to hear your voice again! I'll get straight to business – we can catch up with the small talk later. I believe you've met DCI Patricia McMahon of the Fraud Squad? Well, she's been contacting stations along the south coast, including Brighton, and she thought she might include Woodhampton, since she's an old friend of mine – we worked together several years ago on a big real-estate scam here. What she told me was that your current case has drawn her attention to a certain Signor Passarella, aka Charlie Parsons, who is currently masquerading as a paint salesman, and she wants to set up a programme of surveillance on him and the small businesses that he is dealing with – some are legitimate, but most are covers for criminal activity, she suspects. She hasn't got the numbers of staff to do very much herself, so she is calling upon those stations along this part of the coast who are big enough to have CID departments. I said I could assign at least three people from Woodhampton, providing it was not for too lengthy a period and they were not needed by us for more urgent cases."

Melpomene asked, "So, the idea is not to pick him up, but to use him as bait for bigger fish?"

"That's Pat McMahon's plan – she is working hand-in-glove with the drug squad on this. As well as drugs and gun-running, she reckons that there is a widespread organization behind many of the money transfers to do with illicit stock and share trading. No doubt she'll share her plans with you and Alex, so I don't need to go into any more details, Mel. So how's life in the metropolis, generally? Any other interesting cases, or is this one taking up most of your time?"

Mel chatted with him for a while and then said, "Mama tells me that Stephen Buckmaster is there this evening – maybe I could have a word with him as well."

The conversation that ensued was largely social but after a while, Mel said, "Stephen, are you still in touch with Lionel Sharpe? I want to find out about some embassy matters, and he might be the best person to ask first of all, given his connections with the St Luke's embassy. The comptroller there was Cyril Sidmouth at the time of our enquiries, but he has since been put away on charges of embezzlement and illicit money transactions! It's possible that Lionel knows the comptroller at the Italian embassy, or can put us onto someone reliable in the know – we don't want to risk disclosing our interest to somebody who might be involved in wrong-doing."

"Let me see, I should have his telephone number – yes, here we are, have you got something to write with? Although my daughter Phoebe and Janice Sharpe are still close friends, I haven't spoken with Lionel for a few weeks now – last I heard was that he was waiting for a new posting, since he doesn't want to have anything to do with St Luke's after the upheavals there. Anyway, that's his home number, so someone should answer even if he's in at the Foreign Office – but that reminds me, didn't you get some help from that friend of Adrian Fitz-Hugh's, Sir Howard Anderson, last time? He might even be a better adviser for your present purposes than Lionel Sharpe."

"Thanks for that, Stephen – I think you are right, so tomorrow we'll see what he says. We'd better let you and the other guests go to dinner now – please give my Mama our apologies!"

Alex, who, of course had been listening on the extension, agreed with Mel that this might be well worth following up, "I've been in some doubt as to what you'll be able to find out using your false identity as tutor, but Howard might be able to suggest different approaches, especially if he and Patricia McMahon's people have uncovered further links between those engaged in illicit currency transactions and embassy staff like Scarletta."

"That will all have to wait until tomorrow, Alex, I'm completely bushed now – all I want to do after dinner is to quieten my mind with a therapeutic crossword puzzle, have a bath and go to bed with a mug of hot chocolate or Horlicks!"

So it was not until Melpomene and Alex had got to the office, and briefed the secretaries about the previous evening's call to Lady Cynthia at Woodhampton Castle Hotel, that they started planning a programme of telephone calls.

"Jimmy Manley first, I think," said Alex, "I want to know whether he and any of his Mile End Road staff will be involved in the surveillance along the south coast. Then, we'll see whether Pat McMahon has caught Passarella up to any tricks as Charlie Parsons, and then we can talk to Howard Anderson. And when I was shaving this morning Mel – I don't know what prompted this – I thought that I'd remind you again of the danger of Pellegrini recognising you from your encounter in the street. You're dressed differently in your schoolteacher outfit these days, with glasses and that fetching auburn hair, but it's mannerisms that often give people away."

Jimmy was in his office when they rang, and told them, "I wanted to keep involved, so I've sent Cec and his wife and children for a wintery week's break at a boarding-house in Brighton. He will report to me daily, and work closely with DCI McMahon and the people at the other stations. This operation has already produced some results, I'm happy to tell you! Only yesterday, a CID man from Hastings, PC Galloway, called at Passarella's digs, ostensibly to enquire about Easter bookings, and was in reception when he saw Passarella – we've circulated photographs to everybody – leave the hotel in earnest conversation with a large man in a mackintosh and sea-boots. Galloway followed, of course at a discreet distance, and saw Passarella and the seaman walk to a rundown collection of sheds close to the pier. He didn't want to get too close, but in any case they were only out of sight inside for a few minutes. Then the two emerged, and Passarella was now carrying a bundle wrapped in oilskin. They shook hands cordially and parted, Passarella coming back to his hotel, and the other heading for a nearby pub, apparently a favourite bar for fishermen and other seafarers. Galloway went in, but he couldn't spot the seaman among the throng inside, so he went back to Brighton station and reported."

"Very interesting!" said Melpomene, "It's interesting to speculate about the contents of that bundle, but I can't imagine how we could inspect it without blowing the whole exercise!"

Chapter 43

Jimmy Manley said, "Pat McMahon thinks that the package either contains cash, or more likely bearer bonds or other negotiable securities, and the hand-over to Passarella that was spotted is one step on its journey from a European source to a spurious account in the English branch of a continental bank, such as Banca Popolare di Palermo, which we suspect has been set up by someone in Perrin and Wesley or Castelbianco, perhaps by Passarella himself. Presumably there will be a matching transaction in the reverse direction, since these people don't trust deals based solely on paper-work. So our observers will keep their eyes open for a courier travelling by speed-boat or other small craft. The fact that the bundle was wrapped in waterproof materials gives a clue to this type of journey, and we know that speed-boats have been used frequently by the mobs for cross-channel gun-running and the like. I have to go now, Mel, but as soon as I find out anything relevant, I'll pass it on to you – have fun!"

Mel thanked Jimmy and turned to Alex, "We should try to telephone Archie Staples now – he said he had something interesting for us. We'll try his chambers first – could you get the number for me, please, Marjorie."

The chambers clerk answered the telephone and said that Staples KC was taking instructions from a solicitor at that moment, but would be asked to ring back as soon as he was free. In the event, this was less than twenty minutes later, and Archie greeted Melpomene cheerily.

"You may have heard that Ronald Sedgwick has been arrested by the Fraud Squad and will be facing several charges of embezzlement and falsification of the books at Perrin and Wesley. I am not engaged for this action, but another barrister in these chambers, Gerald Ponsonby, KC, is going to be defending him. He acted in an earlier case in which Sedgwick and others were accused of failure to act in the best interests of a client – you may remember that I found this for you when you were first looking for dirt on Perrin and Wesley. Ponsonby must have impressed Sedgwick then, so he's being called again this time! Apart from it just being interesting, I think there may be further advantages to be gained here – I happen to know that Sedgwick's solicitor, Edwin Tweedie, is a rather shifty individual who gets very loquacious when in his cups, and might be a useful source of information about Sedgwick's associates, including Commodore Lane, who seems to have been a close pal, though I believe he's disavowed it since the arrest."

"And you think," said Mel, "that this Tweedie character can be used to expose how Sedgwick is involved at deeper levels of this criminal fraternity? If he's as shifty as you say, surely he'll twig what's going on if we try to pump him?"

"Not if we get him suitably sozzled – not a difficult task if my information is accurate! What I was going to suggest is that one or both of you bump into me accidentally in a pub I know he frequents, and we gossip among ourselves, and then invite Tweedie to join us and ply him a bit with whatever he's drinking at the time – I'm told he rather likes pink gins. Then we carry on with our chat, mentioning a name or two we're interested in, and see what happens. It's my bet that he will not be able to resist airing his inside knowledge! Worth a try?"

"I'm game!" said Melpomene without hesitation, and Alex, who had of course been listening, immediately agreed.

"Right you are! How about tomorrow at just after six? My inside informant tells me that he is practically always to be found straight after work in the saloon bar of the Five Bells in Wickham Street, near the Inns of Court – do you know where that is, Alex? Wonderful – see you then!"

Melpomene said, "We did intend to speak to Pat McMahon, but Jimmy has already told us quite a lot about the incident with Passarella, so maybe we might be better off talking to Howard Anderson at the Foreign Office next – could you try his number for me please, Marjorie?"

There was the usual delay before Anderson's somewhat snooty secretary could be persuaded to bother the great man, but as soon as he spoke, he said, "Please excuse Miss Thornton, Melpomene, she does a great job protecting me from trivial matters, but of course I'm always very happy to speak to you or Alex. How can I help this time?"

Mel gave him a brief account of the present case, ending by saying, "We are uncertain whether or not staff at the Italian embassy might be involved to any extent in dubious financial transactions, and of course we can't just go ahead and ask anyone at random, in case we alert the guilty parties, if any there are. So we turn to you, Howard, for your advice."

"You did right, Mel, diplomacy is a very sensitive area anyway, and to raise the question of irregular behaviour of embassy staff would be tantamount to precipitating an international incident – and relations between Great Britain and Italy are only just settling down after the disruption of the War! Do you actually suspect anyone at the embassy in particular?"

"Only by implication, Howard, as I'll mention in a moment, but we know of a man called Gian Carlo Passarella, who has a long record of involvement with drug and gun running and the associated financial dealings that go along with those. Your Home Office colleague and friend, Adrian Fitz-Hugh, has assigned some of his staff, and a member of the Fraud Squad, DCI Patricia McMahon, to keep a close eye on him, and he can be picked up whenever it seems appropriate, but of course we're all hoping he'll lead us to other members of the ring. We already know that he has a close relationship with Osvaldo Scarletta, aka Griguolo, who is a known member of Embassy staff – by the way, I've been tutoring his little daughter in English, along with a few other embassy children – but that's another story, which I'll relate to you another time!"

"Very well, Melpomene, what I'm going to do now is to set my specialist staff to perusing their records for anything referring to the Italian embassy. We routinely note all mentions of foreign embassies and their personnel, whether they are simply news items in the press, or complaints received from the public about high-handed behaviour of Visa clerks, or in fact anything at all. We have a fairly sophisticated series of protocols for organising all this information, involving the use of punched cards, so we can search on any key word or combination of words. I can say with some pride that our installation has become a model for many others – mind you, we don't reveal all the tricks we have developed! We work very closely with the Hollerith company in the States, which has just recently been renamed International Business Machines. Some day, when you're not busy with a case, I'll get one of our staff to demonstrate what we can do. Sorry about that – I tend to wax enthusiastic about all this!"

"That sounds very good, Howard, when will you be able to give us the results of your searches – does it take days, or what?"

129

Chapter 44

Howard Anderson was clearly rather proud of his contraption –
as he told Melpomene, "I'm very happy to disabuse you of that
pessimistic view! Our Hollerith system, far from taking days to
make a search, can usually spit out a series of cards listing the
documents of interest within half an hour! Then our clerks can
locate the items searched for within a further twenty minutes or
so – we are very well organized here! This time, I'll get the
operator to do a general search for all references to the Italian
embassy – we don't have anything tagged as 'legal' or 'illegal',
so you'll just have to use your judgment and your knowledge
of the situation as you go through the resulting documents.
Would you be free to come here to do that at, say, two o'clock
this afternoon? Right-oh, I'll literally get the wheels turning
straight away!"

"Thanks very much Howard, we'll see you then!"

Melpomene said, "I don't know about the rest of you, but I'm
about ready for lunch – let's go to Guiseppe's, as I'm getting a
bit bored with sandwiches and pork pies!"

"If you don't mind," said Marjorie, "I won't accompany you
this time, Mel. I have my Mum's packed lunch and anyway
someone needs to stay and mind the office and answer the
telephone."

The others piled into the Riley and were soon sitting down to a
meal at the trattoria, which, as always, didn't disappoint. Alex
decided that he would pass on the wine, as he was driving, but
Melpomene and Winnie shared a carafe of Sangiovese.

But all too soon, Alex consulted his wristwatch and said, "Time
to go to see what Howard Anderson has got for us. It's
fortunate that you are with us, Winnie, because you're very
good at sorting through documents and you are also *au fait*
with our concerns about the embassy."

At the anonymous Home Office building, they were recognized
by the man at the reception counter, who waved them toward
the lifts with a cheery smile. Soon, an attendant took them to a
long table where there were several folders of documents.

"My name is Florrie Hattersley. If you wish to speak to Sir
Howard, please ask me – he is in a meeting, but he told me he's

willing to be disturbed. Meanwhile, I have to stay in the room, because of regulations, so if you need any help, please say so."

Melpomene, Alex and Winnie took a folder each and started leafing through the documents, which seemed to be a mixture of originals and photostats. There was silence for a few minutes, then Winnie exclaimed, "Have a look at this, Mel and Alex!" and held up a bundle of what appeared to be copies of telegrams, fastened together with paperclips.

Mel took the bundle and started to read through it. When she had finished, she said, "This is the record of the cable correspondence between someone called Ernesto Marchetti and two officials of the Italian embassy, one of whose names rings a bell with us – Osvaldo Scarletta! How about that? The cables are in Italian, so I don't have a clear picture of the content – we shall have to get a linguist to interpret for us – but I did spot a few words or phrases that look interesting. One of them was *'Banca Popolare di Palermo'* and another was *'Guardia di Finanza'*, which, if memory serves me right, was mentioned by Hortense Deslarges as the Italian government body that oversees customs matters."

"So," said Alex, "the inference one can draw, pending having these properly translated, is that they deal with financial matters. And one would think that if they were entirely legitimate, they would be the responsibility of someone other than dear Osvaldo – the comptroller for instance – do we know who he is?"

"I can tell you that!" said Winnie, "the next folder I looked at had notepaper with the Italian crest and the heading *'Piero Gambaro, Primo Consigliere per gli affari economici e commerciali'*, which doesn't take much guesswork!"

Florrie, the attendant, who had been sitting near the door, spoke up at this point, "I couldn't help hearing you talk about translating – I have a colleague here, Annette Bingham, who is fairly fluent in Italian, and could certainly give you the gist of whatever documents particularly interest you – shall I fetch her? It won't take long, she's on this floor, and I'm sure she'll welcome a break in whatever she's been doing this afternoon!"

Five minutes later, Florrie brought her friend in, and Winnie showed her the bundle of telegrams, which she flipped through quite quickly.

"They are all along the same lines," she said, "each of them amounts to a request by one or other of the embassy officials, Scarletta or Danielo, for Signor Marchetti to initiate the transfer of funds from a bank in Italy – there were three or four different ones named – to specific accounts, identified only by number, in the local branch of Banca Popolare di Palermo. I should point out that these transactions will already have been checked by our staff, in collaboration with DCI McMahon of the Fraud Squad, who is liaising both with us and Sir Adrian Fitz-Hugh's unit at the Home Office. These reports, I should point out, are kept separately, and not entered into our general filing system, so the Hollerith search will not have found them. Maybe Sir Howard will authorize their disclosure to you."

Melpomene thanked Annette, and said, "If you're not in a hurry to return to your office, perhaps you could also give us the gist of the letters in this folder of correspondence, which have the air of being rather more legitimate, as they are from and to the senior council for economic and commercial affairs."

"Let me see," said Annette, "by the way, I'm certainly in no hurry to get back to my desk – I've been doing really boring stuff all day! These are about money transfers, too, the difference being that they concern dealings between the embassy's official account here at the Bank of England, and that of the Italian equivalent in Rome of our Foreign Office, the *Ministero degli Affari Esteri*. I would say that these transactions are legitimate and so wouldn't be of interest to your enquiries – but you'd better check with Sir Howard as I'm but a lowly minion!"

"Don't sell yourself short, my dear!" said Melpomene, "Please help us go through the remaining documents that have been thrown up by your magic machine. We've already had our attention directed to a new suspect, this Signor Danielo – we haven't run into him before. And we must certainly see what can be found out about Ernesto Marchetti – by the way, what is given as his address in the telegrams?"

"I'll look – oh, it's a telegraphic address, so some senior person will have to apply to the Post Office to find what destination it represents. I'm sure that Sir Howard can organize this for you."

"You wouldn't consider changing careers, would you, Annette?" said Mel "We could do with someone like you in our agency – only kidding!"

Chapter 45

After a further hour going through the documents, Alex announced that they had probably seen and noted all the interesting points they were going to find at this sitting. He thanked Annette for her help and asked Florrie if she would check whether Sir Howard was still occupied or was free for a chat.

It was not long before he came into the room, smiling and saying, "Good afternoon, Mel and Alex, and I'm pleased to meet Miss Morris, too – we've spoken on the telephone several times, but it's nice to put a face to the voice! Now Florence Ferguson has just told me that your time here seems to have been fruitful – I assume that this means that you have discovered some facts that will be useful for your case, is that right?"

"Certainly, Howard," said Melpomene, "we have come across a few additional names to add to our list of suspects at the embassy, as well as one or two people elsewhere, who seem to have been involved in dealings that look a bit suspicious to us. Annette Bingham – who was very helpful too – tells us that your people may have already identified some illicit transactions and that this information would not have been included in the documents we have just seen. Would you feel free to share this with us, if it seems relevant to our case?"

"Yes, with certain reservations, Melpomene – particularly as it mentions the names of His Excellency the Ambassador himself, and two of his senior attaches – we would need you, Alex and Miss Morris to sign a non-disclosure agreement. If you were to violate the terms of this agreement, the penalties would be severe, ranging up to imprisonment! If I might suggest a strategy to you all, the safest approach would be never to commit any of these names to writing, and never to say them aloud in the hearing of others."

Howard asked Florrie to bring in the relevant forms, and all three signed them and had their signatures witnessed.

"I do apologize for all this formality, but it is unavoidable when one is dealing with diplomatic matters," said Sir Howard, "now I can tell you all about it. You already know that after investigations by Adrian Fitz-Hugh's people, in collaboration with the Fraud Squad, and Mlle Deslarges at the Sûreté, it was possible to arrest Ronald Sedgwick – a matter of considerable satisfaction to your client, Mr Hotchkiss, I imagine. What you probably do not yet know is that a high official at the Italian embassy was also thought to be involved. We are having to tread carefully here, as we do whenever diplomats are suspected, but since you three have signed a non-disclosure agreement, I'm able to tell you that the official is Signor Piero Gambaro, First Counseller for economic and financial affairs. If we supply the Foreign Secretary with sufficient proof, Gambaro can be declared *persona non grata* so losing his diplomatic protected status and enabling him to be arrested and charged with violating British laws. The necessary procedures are under way, but have not yet reached a conclusion."

"This is all very encouraging, Howard!" said Melpomene, "Can you say whether there are prospects of further arrests? We know that Sedgwick had accomplices at Perrin and Wesley, including a Peter Walsh, and Patricia McMahon told us that Sir William Carr-Hazelton and Felix Cattermole had been taken in for questioning, but released later – and we're aware that the names of Commodore Lane and Sylvia Myers have come up more than once – have Scotland Yard or the Sûreté identified anyone else lately? It looks as though Patricia's team will be swooping on Gian Carlo Passarella quite soon, and he might lead us to others, unless Omertà, the Mafia code of silence, is as powerful as it is reputed to be."

"You'll have to ask Adrian Fitz-Hugh about those things, Melpomene, we've got enough on our plates dealing with the diplomatic side. I'll make sure you are informed when anything that concerns you comes up, meanwhile, I suggest your best links are with the Home Office and the police – and maybe your contacts over the Channel. I'm glad that you found your visit here worthwhile – it's always a pleasure for me to talk to you!"

On their way back to the office, Winnie said, "Well, that was very interesting – it's made me wonder if anything has been happening with Passarella while we've been busy – should we telephone Jimmy as soon as we get in, to see if he knows anything yet?"

So, as soon as they reached the agency and had filled their immediate need for jam tarts and tea, Melpomene tried the CID office at Mile End Road station. The telephone was answered by WPC Dulcie Jarvis, who said, "You've just missed Jimmy – he's on his way to Brighton in response to an urgent call – Cec Thomson has got himself shot! Before you panic too much, it was only a flesh wound from a small-calibre pistol, so he's going to be all right!"

"Goodness gracious!" said Mel, "How did that happen – was it Passarella or what?"

"Yes, it was, Melpomene – Cec and a team of local police, following orders from DCI McMahon, made sure that Gian Carlo was alone in his digs, then moved in to arrest him. This was first thing this morning – but apparently Passarella decided he wouldn't cooperate and took a couple of pot-shots at them, winging Cec before some of the others managed to wrestle his pistol away and overcome him!"

"So, Dulcie, after all that excitement, I imagine that Jimmy won't be back at the station today – could you please leave a note for him that Alex and I would appreciate hearing from him at his convenience – we're going home to our flat now, and we'll come to the office at our usual time tomorrow morning."

Melpomene related this story to the others, who were suitably astonished, and then said "Well that's it for today for us! Maybe tomorrow we shall be able to start planning what to do with all the information we got from Howard today. Before we leave, were there any telephone calls while we were away, Marjorie? I was intending to ring Archie Staples and let him know I mightn't be able to keep our appointment tomorrow evening, depending on what comes up from the Passarella incident. I think it's a bit late to catch him in chambers now, so I might try his home number this evening. So if by any chance he should call before you two knock off, you could tell him that. Don't stay too long, and we'll see you in the morning."

Marjorie said, "Take these with you to read over dinner!" and handed Alex two long envelopes, "I think they look like summonses or something else of a legal nature – they were delivered by courier only a few minutes before you got here, so I haven't had a chance to open them yet."

"Very intriguing!" said Alex, "I wonder what we've done now? My conscience is reasonably clear – maybe Mel hasn't returned her library books, or the council rates are overdue or something!"

Chapter 46

As soon as they reached the flat, they sat down with cups of tea – Mrs Mountain discouraged them from having cake or biscuits, saying "You'll spoil yer dinner, and I done you apricot glazed ham with potatoes and asparagus, so it'd be a pity ter ruin yer appetite!" – and then Alex slit open the two mysterious envelopes. He went quiet for a while, so Melpomene said, "Come on, Alex, put me out of my misery – are they something awful?"

"Not at all Mel – in fact they bring good news of two different sorts! The first is simply to notify us that our gun and ammunition licences are due for renewal, and the second informs us that the Crabbe and Crabbe Agency has been accredited by the Home Office as a 'body ancillary to the Metropolitan Police Service' with a list of the privileges and powers attached to such a body. We are each eligible for a special card, conveying many of the same powers as a standard Met warrant card. There's more, but we can read that at our leisure, I think!"

"Very gratifying!" said Mel, "Even though I suppose it's largely a courtesy matter, rather than anything substantive – we'll ask Adrian Fitz-Hugh about it when we see him next. I suppose we'd better wait until after dinner before we ring Archie Staples, otherwise Mrs M will grumble at us again!"

In the event, they had hardly finished the main course, and were contemplating the prunes and custard which followed, when the telephone rang. It was Jimmy, sounding tired but cheerful, "You'll be glad to know that Cec has been patched up and is sleeping comfortably at the East Brighton cottage hospital, with the aid of some sedatives – I'll bring him and his family home tomorrow. The doctor dug a bullet out of him – it was small, what they call '22 long rifle' calibre, and hadn't gone very deeply into his upper arm. The forensics people will examine it, of course, but I'm guessing it was Passarella's gun that also dispatched Cinzia Preston. This is a very unusual little weapon called a Mossberg Brownie – it has four barrels, each loaded separately, and is very easy to conceal, but has limited effect – unless you press it to the back of someone's head! Gian Carlo Passarella has been arrested, of course, charged for now with assault causing grievous bodily harm – later I'm pretty confident he will be up for the murder of Cinzia Tagliamonte, alias Preston. Deputy Commissioner Fitz-Hugh is insistent that the case be dealt with here in England, no matter what the authorities in Europe say, since Passarella has wriggled out of serious charges in France and Italy more than once before, no doubt with the aid of his Mafia connections."

"This is all good news – thanks, Jimmy! Give our best wishes to Cec when you get a chance, please." said Melpomene, "Tomorrow I'm due to go back to the embassy for my English class, so I'll keep my eyes and ears open in the cafeteria at lunchtime to see whether this arrest has had an impact on anyone there. If any of the staff are involved, they will be covering up, of course, so any signs might be subtle."

Finishing off his prunes and custard, Alex said, "Now we'll see whether we can have a yarn with Archie Staples. I have his home number in my little book. Thanks, Caroline, I'll take my after-dinner coffee at the telephone table."

Archie seemed happy to hear Alex' voice, saying, "I've been waiting in some anticipation to give you an item of information, which, if I'm any judge, you might find very valuable to your case. You remember I told you about that solicitor, Edwin Tweedie? The one that we had planned to get squiffy and pump about Sedgwick's activities and associates? Well, that won't be possible now, because he's vanished! The other people in my chambers who I feel safe talking to reckon that he's simply done a bunk, but I've got a strange feeling that he's been eliminated by the mob, either bumped off or kidnapped!"

"What makes you think this way, Archie?"

"Listen to what I found out about his recent behaviour and see what you think! One of our junior clerks, Stan Figgis, was sent to his office by Gerald Ponsonby to fetch him some documents bearing on the Sedgwick case, and was greeted affably by Tweedie, who engaged him in conversation about his local football side, who recently, I'm told, has had a notable victory over a long-standing rival. The point is that Edwin Tweedie was obviously in a relaxed mood – hardly a sign that he was planning to disappear voluntarily. Then when young Stan got back to chambers, he realized he'd left an important deposition behind, so he rang the solicitor's office to ask Mr Tweedie to keep it for him until he could get back to collect it. The girl who answered said she would look after that, but that he couldn't speak to Tweedie, because he had just left in a hurry with two rather large scary men in overcoats who she didn't recognize. Sounds fishy, does it not?"

"It certainly does, Archie! We know that these gangs are not averse to using violence to ensure that no damaging information gets out – there have already been two murders that we attribute to this." said Alex, "Did you try to follow this up?"

"Well, I did, and asked the girl if she noticed anything else about these men, but she couldn't tell me much, except that the one that seemed to be in charge said something to his mate that sounded like 'handy armour' – I wondered whether it was 'andiamo', which is Italian for 'let's go'!"

"Good guessing, Archie – we are convinced that there is an Italian connection to all of this – I won't say much more but we're certainly following up this line. You'll be amused to hear that Melpomene has infiltrated the Italian embassy, heavily disguised as a red-headed language tutor, to try to find out what might be going on. We'll keep you informed, Archie, meanwhile it might be interesting if you could keep an eye on the activities of Gerald Ponsonby, KC, since he's a member of your chambers – he might well be interviewing some of Sedgwick's associates in preparing his defence."

"Good idea, Alex – he is rather inclined to leave a lot of the details to the chambers clerks, and I'm on good terms with most of them, like Stan Figgis. They would know all about outgoing and incoming correspondence, and although they don't listen to telephone calls, they would know the names of frequent callers – I'll have to be fairly discreet, of course."

"We're very grateful for your efforts on our behalf, Archie – we'll try to make it up to you some time – if we come across a useful informant from the criminal fraternity who needs legal representation, perhaps!"

"Don't be too concerned, Alex – I'm not exactly over-burdened with work these days, but I am getting known by more and more solicitors, so business might pick up before long. Give my regards to Melpomene and let her know that I hope that she'll be able to discover something useful at the embassy."

"Certainly, Archie – when things settle down we might be able to squeeze in a round or two of golf! Our regards to Betty, too!"

138

Chapter 47

Alex went back into the living-room and told Mel what Archie had said, adding, "We shouldn't bother Jimmy about that tonight, Mel, it sounds as though he had a very busy, even trying, day. In the morning I'll tell him about the apparent abduction and he can follow it up if he thinks it'll be worthwhile. Now I'm ready for my bath and bed!"

"What are your plans for tomorrow, Alex? No – don't tell me now, otherwise you'll be thinking about them all night! I'm going to the embassy to introduce my kids to Rupert Bear and then, after the lesson, I'll see whether Signorina Primavera Guzzi has heard anything new."

Alex seemed to be preoccupied all through breakfast, and as they were driving to the office, he said, "I've decided to pay another visit to Perrin and Wesley today – I thought I'd take the bit between my teeth and start asking some direct questions. I believe the time has passed for being too cautious – nevertheless I shall still stick to my cover as someone wanting to explore the prospects for switching my career from the law to finance. If I see any of the people we've got earmarked as doubtful, I shall just blunder ahead and ask them naive questions, mainly to see whether and in what ways they react."

As they were walking in the door, Melpomene said, "I'm not sure I understood what you had in mind as your naive questions – can you give me an example, Alex?"

"I'll tell you just as soon as I've had a cup of tea and a jam tart! – Good morning, Marjorie and Winnie – what's new since we saw you last? By the way, we heard from Jimmy last night that Cec Thomson has been patched up and will be fine soon, so that's a relief!"

"The postman hasn't been yet, and there have been no telephone calls this morning, so we've got precious little to report – and what were those legal-looking letters we gave you as you left yesterday?"

"Here's the first one, Marjorie, if you wouldn't mind dealing with it for us – it's the renewal for our guns and ammo permits, that's all. And the other one is rather inspiring, since it says that the Home Office has accredited Crabbe and Crabbe as a 'body ancillary to the Metropolitan Police Service' – so you two will have the pleasant duty of getting the document framed and displayed on the office wall with our other degree certificates and so on – we shall soon convey a truly professional aura!"

After a little more chat, Melpomene said, "As I asked you in the car, Alex – what sort of naive questions have you in mind?"

"I shall have to extemporize, actually, but I can give you a taste – suppose I find myself next to the notorious Commodore Lane. I could say to him something along the lines of 'Oh, Commodore, I hear that your friend Mr Sedgwick is in big trouble – will you be able to put in a good word for him with the authorities?' Then I shall see whether he persists in saying he was never a friend, or whether he wriggles out some other way."

"Or flatly tells you it's none of your business and punches you in the nose! We've been told that Lane's not averse to violence! Have you other targets in mind?"

"There's your pal Sylvia Myers for a start, and there's this Peter Walsh, though I don't know much about him. Patricia McMahon also mentioned that Sir William Carr-Hazelton and Felix Cattermole were questioned as suspects, but were let go for want of evidence, so they might be good candidates for me. What I'll do is have a good chat with Eric Hotchkiss first and get his views on this approach. I think it's a bit early to try telephoning him now, but I think I should alert him before I go there. I'll need a reason for my visit to P and W, anyway – I can't just breeze in off the street."

Melpomene remembered a thought she'd had earlier, "You know, Alex, so far we've done nothing about Castelbianco – they might be worth a visit, since we know that Osvaldo Griguolo, aka Scarletta, is reputed to work there as well as at the embassy."

"Right, Mel, but I'd have to devise an excuse for a visit there, too – I'll think about it, and Eric might have ideas as well. I'll telephone him after 10 o'clock, when he should be at his desk."

"Good, Alex – I shall be gone by then, because I go to the embassy by tube, and my class starts at ten o'clock. It finishes at noon, and then my real work will start!"

"Oh, Mel, let me remind you to watch out for that man, Antonio Pellegrini, the one you had an altercation with on the street near the Old Street post office – he might not recognise you the way you look now, but don't take any chances!"

At the embassy, Mel's class greeted her warmly – little Gerardo Ferrero even plucked up the courage to say "very good morning, teacher", although Mel suspected he might have been coached by his brother, Rafaello. After a few minutes of general conversation, the Rupert Bear strips were brought out and Mel was relieved to find that they went down very well, so that the children were sorry once again when the class ended at noon. Rosa Scarletta even insisted on kissing Mel goodbye!

By that time, Melpomene was feeling rather peckish, so she headed to the cafeteria and ordered a potato and prosciutto frittata, which looked substantial enough to keep her going for a while. She looked around for a familiar face, but found no-one she could approach, so sat at a table by the windows and thought of ways she might introduce herself.

But then she was saved the trouble, when Mrs Abbott, carrying a loaded tray, came over and said, "Can I join you, Mrs Musgrave? How was your class this morning?"

"Oh, it went very well, thank you – I can see some improvement in one or two of the children already, and they seem to have accepted me. I'd like to remind you that I want to speak to some other parents if I can – I've already spoken to Signor Scarletta and Signor Ponzi, but they don't seem to be here today."

"I'm sure I'll be able to arrange that soon, Mrs Musgrave, but I ought to explain that many of the senior and middle-level officers are attending a meeting called by His Excellency, to follow up the visit here a couple of days ago of a principal Police Commissioner and members of the Foreign Office – we've just broken for lunch, but most of the attachés have stayed in the formal dining-room upstairs for that, at the request of the ambassador – I was thought not to be important enough to join them there, it seems! The parents you've not met, Silvio Manfredi and Rinaldo Ferrero, are both concerned with this enquiry, which has been set up by His Excellency as a result of serious allegations about financial transactions which indirectly affect the embassy. Of course, the whole place is seething with rumours, and some rather nasty accusations are starting to emerge – mostly unfounded, but perhaps that is merely my own wishful thinking!"

Chapter 48

"Fascinating!" said Melpomene, "Has anybody been directly accused, either by the police or by the Foreign Office? Are you permitted to tell me the names of the officials who visited?"

"I only heard one name, Mrs Musgrave – Commissioner Fitz-Hugh, from Scotland Yard, who was introduced to us by HE – but the Foreign Office people, three of them, were playing their cards close to their chests – they didn't even use names when they were talking among themselves, as far as I could tell."

"Commissioner Fitz-Hugh, you say? That rank sounds fairly senior, so Scotland Yard must be taking this seriously. Did he or the FO types specifically accuse any officers of the embassy?"

"Not as such, but I noticed that Signor Piero Gambaro was looking very uncomfortable – he's in charge of economic and financial affairs here, so it's likely that his staff would have to be involved in any major financial transactions, and he might have to carry the can for their irregularities."

"What was the nature of these irregularities, Mrs Abbot, was this disclosed at all, or were they just being vague?"

"Please call me Dorothy, Mrs Musgrave, and maybe I can use your first name, too – it's Hettie, isn't it? I'm pretty naive when it comes to finance – it's as much as I can do to manage my own household budget – but what I picked up from the discussion was that even legitimate businesses want to keep major transactions secret, because their rivals would gain an advantage from knowing about them. I was sitting next to one of the officers who deal with money transfers back and forth between the Rome government and our embassy, and he explained it to me, saying that using the embassy for hidden transactions would mean that a firm could steal a march on its competitors!"

"Did he say that this was the reason for the enquiry – is there someone at the embassy doing this on the quiet?"

"He seemed to suddenly realize he was being indiscreet in talking to me, and quickly changed the subject! But later on in the proceedings, Signor Gambaro made a long statement, saying that he was confident that nothing untoward was going on in his area of responsibility. But the men from the Foreign

Office looked meaningfully at one another as he spoke, so I feel that he's in it up to his neck!"

"That's all very fascinating, Dorothy," said Melpomene, "but nothing one could really get hold of, so far. What's going to happen when the meeting is reconvened after lunch, did they say? Oh, I'd so like to be a fly on the wall – not that it's any real business of mine!"

"I believe that, after everyone who wants to has made a contribution, the Scotland Yard man and the most senior Foreign Office person are going to make statements, so they could be rather interesting – will you be able to hang about to hear what I have to say afterwards, or have you got to go home, Hettie?"

"I'm afraid that I'll have to go soon, but I'm terribly grateful you have told me all this – I hope you won't get into any trouble!"

"I don't think so – I'm one of those people who merge into the background, much like part of the furniture – you wouldn't believe some of the things I've been told in confidence, especially when people have had a couple of drinks!"

Dorothy Abbot looked at the clock, excused herself and headed out with a cheerful wave, as a man in a suit came into the cafeteria and rang a little bell for attention.

"My apologies for disturbing you, ladies and gentlemen, but His Excellency the Ambassador, Conte Lorenzetti, has called everyone to the main banquet hall for important announcements. Please make your way there as quickly as possible."

Mel purposely avoided asking her companions whether she should come too, thinking to herself, "I'm a legitimate employee, after all!"

They joined a stream of people on the staircase and soon entered the banquet room. Some people were still seated, but most, including the newcomers were lining the walls, looking expectantly toward the raised dais, where three men were standing ready.

Melpomene saw that Primavera was already in the hall, so she went and joined her. She could also see Dorothy Abbott ahead of them, standing quite close to the stage – she was wearing a tailored suit, and carrying a handbag in her left hand, with her right hand buried in the side pocket of the jacket – she seemed to be fidgeting nervously for some reason.

When it seemed that there were no more people entering the hall, a thickset balding man stepped forward. Primavera murmured to Mel, "Signor Bocalli, the Deputy *Chef de Mission*", as the man called for silence, saying, "His Excellency, Conte Lorenzetti, L'Ambasciatore d'Italia, will address you in English, as many of the staff are local employees."

The ambassador, tall, spare and silver-haired, proceeded to speak in a clear voice, audible even at the back of the room.

"Ladies and gentlemen, colleagues and associates, my duty compels me to make this speech with a heavy heart. Two of our most valued officers have disappointed me profoundly by their actions, which have endangered the work and the very reputation of our embassy, and by implication, of our dear motherland. I am deeply ashamed to name them, to declare them *personae non gratae*, and to call upon them to surrender themselves to the English civil authorities. I refer to Signor Piero Gambaro, our First Counseller for Economic and Financial Affairs, and a member of his staff, Signor Osvaldo Scarletta. Would they please stand up and come to me here, and I will explain further."

There was a buzz of excited chatter throughout the hall, as the two disgraced persons hesitantly made their way toward the stage. At the same time, four men, clearly plain-clothes police, left their places against the wall and positioned themselves ready, evidently to take the two into custody.

The disgraced men, walking rather reluctantly, but glancing warily at the plain-clothed men on each side of the hall, had nearly reached the dais, when Scarletta suddenly drew a pistol and pointed it at the Ambassador, shouting, "I'm going to leave now – if anyone tries to stop me, His Excellency is a dead man!"

He had hardly finished uttering this threat when shots rang out and he pitched forward onto the raised edge of the platform, his revolver clattering away across the floor. The audience uttered a gasp as Scarletta started to scream in pain, apparently wounded in the shoulder and leg, but conscious enough to utter a stream of profanities!

144

Chapter 49

As a general astonished babble broke out in the audience, a figure familiar to Melpomene, Sir Adrian Fitz-Hugh, took the centre of the stage and called for silence, "Ladies and gentlemen, an ambulance has been called – this would-be assassin's wounds will be attended to first, before he and his companion are taken into custody. Then, I would appeal to everyone present to cooperate with the police officers who will be taking eye-witness statements. There is already some confusion over the number of shots that were fired, and by whom, and we need to sort this out properly before first impressions are overtaken by second thoughts. There are too many people assembled here for us to interrogate everyone in detail, so I would suggest that you only contribute if you have something to report that you feel may be significant, otherwise please leave this hall, leaving your name with the officers at the door."

As everyone started to move toward the exits, Melpomene wondered what she would say, thinking that giving the police a false name might make her liable to be charged. So when she faced an officer, she was relieved to hear him say quietly, "We know who you are, so you needn't perjure yourself – please telephone DCI Manley at your earliest convenience!"

"As it happens, I believe I have a piece of important information in connection with the shooting – should I tell you or save it for Jimmy Manley? It is not immediately urgent."

"Please save it for the DCI, then – but thanks for letting me know. If he asks, I'm DS Willis, from Commissioner Fitz-Hugh's unit."

Melpomene left the embassy then, threading her way past knots of people on the stairs and in the lobbies, all chattering and gesticulating as they discussed what had happened. She made her way to the tube and within half an hour was at the office.

Alex was still out, but of course Marjorie and Winnie were enthralled by Mel's account of the excitement at the embassy.

145

"But I must talk to Jimmy Manley very soon!" she said, as she gratefully accepted a cup of tea and a jam tart, "Please see if he's at Mile End Road station for me, Winnie."

He wasn't there at first, but soon came to the telephone and spoke to Mel – explaining that Scarletta had been taken to hospital, and that Jimmy was going to be involved in interviewing him, once he had been patched up and was ready.

"All he's got is a couple of flesh wounds, but he's making a lot of fuss, even though he's been given strong pain-killers. I hung around until they'd dug the bullets out – I'm a bit puzzled, since one looked like standard police issue, while the other was a small-calibre job, similar to the ones we've retrieved from poor Cecil Thomson and the late Cinzia Preston. The gun that Scarletta was brandishing at the embassy was a Mossberg Brownie, like the one that Passarella used on those two. Of course, Scarletta never got a chance to fire it at the ambassador, since someone unknown shot him in the leg, while one of our men was getting him in the shoulder. Very puzzling! Perhaps they are standard issue for these gang members!"

Melpomene said, "I may be able to add to this, Jimmy – I was keeping my eye on a woman who I felt suspicious about, who I'd been talking with earlier in the cafeteria. Most people in the room were staring in fascination at Scarletta waving his gun about, but I saw Dorothy Abbot firing with her hand still in her pocket, just as he pitched forward, possibly as the police bullet hit him in the shoulder, so it's hard to know where she was aiming – she actually got him in the leg, as it turned out. What I reckon is that she wanted to shut him up, permanently!"

"I think you may be right, Melpomene – he'll be a threat to his organization now we've got our hands on him. Steps have already been taken to make sure he's safely guarded while in custody in the hospital – after losing Angelo Serotti and Cinzia Preston, we didn't want any other potential informants to be eliminated that way! And the same precautions should now be applied to Mrs Abbott, once we've taken her in for interrogation – but we can't just go into a foreign embassy and seize her, so we might have to wait until she goes home. Would you be willing to point her out to some of my men, Mel?"

She agreed, telling Jimmy that she had seen Dorothy Abbot leaving the banquet hall without being stopped, and then they arranged that Mel and a DC would wait opposite the embassy

146

in a tea shop whose windows had a good view up and down the street, at around the time that the staff usually finished work.

Alex returned from Perrin and Wesley's soon after Melpomene had set off – the secretaries told him what had happened at the embassy, and he decided to join Melpomene and her police colleague at the tea shop, saying he might be of help, and anyway didn't want to miss any fun that might be going.

"Has Mel taken her pistol, given that this Mrs Abbott is known to be armed? I've got mine, too, so we should be able to cope. We'll keep an eye on her if her hand seems to be going for her pocket!"

"Before you go, Alex, can you tell us if anything of note happened when you were at Perrin and Wesley?" asked Winnie.

"Certainly – I'm taking the car, so I can afford a few minutes chat! Actually, I'm quite pleased with myself – after I'd seen Eric and told him what I meant to do, he suggested that if I was going to ask leading questions of anybody, I would find that Commodore Lane seemed to be in a very expansive mood today, and that if I were to go to the private bar of the Five Bells I might catch him in a receptive state of mind. Well, to cut a long story short, Winnie and Marjorie, I followed Eric's suggestion and indeed, soon found Lane drinking jovially in the pub with a couple of friends. I approached him and breezily asked him, slurring my speech a little, what mischief he was up to today – this must have hit a sore spot, because he started making aggressive gestures at me and shouting abuse!"

"My word!" said Winnie, "What did you do?"

"Nothing immediately – I was a bit taken aback – and then the barman came and spoke to Lane's companions, telling them to control their friend or he would have to call the police, since the Commodore had created a disturbance once too often. They just made offensive remarks about the barman, whereupon he blew a police whistle, which brought a couple of men – who later turned out to be off-duty detectives – in from the public bar. On the nod from the barman, they seized Lane. What happened next made me feel my efforts at stirring up trouble had been entirely worthwhile! But it's time for me to go now, ladies, so you'll have to contain your curiosity until later, when I'll relate the whole story to you and Mel and the others!"

Chapter 50

Alex soon spotted the tea shop across the street from the embassy, and found Melpomene and a man in plain clothes enjoying cakes and cups of tea at a table near the front window.

He sat down, was introduced to DC Derek Pratt and was told that their quarry had not yet emerged. "Are you sure she'll be coming out of the public entrance?" he asked.

"Yes," said Mel, "because employees, as I've found out, have to sign the attendance book as they leave, and that's kept at the enquiries counter – I think Mrs Abbott would be disinclined to draw attention to herself by doing anything different today. While we're waiting, Alex, you can fill me in on your adventures at P and W, assuming there were some worth reporting."

"Well, I'll let you be the judge of that, Mel! As I had hoped, I managed to confront Commodore Lane and a couple of his associates in the private bar of the Five Bells. I was deliberately provocative and Lane was on a short fuse, so he reacted aggressively – fortunately the barman was ready for this and blew his police whistle, which brought in a couple of off-duty coppers from the public bar. They first warned him, and when he ignored this they laid hands on him and applied their handcuffs! Meanwhile, one of Lane's two mates made a major tactical error, turning what would have been a fairly minor case of disturbing the peace into a more serious incident!"

Both Melpomene and DC Pratt were leaning forward, entranced, Mel saying, "Come on, Alex, don't keep us in suspense – what happened next?"

"I think the larger of Lane's friends must have forgotten he was in England and resorted to behaviour more suited to Sicily or Calabria – he pulled out a large knife and brandished it, shrieking imprecations in what I assume was Italian or a dialect – but he was soon disarmed – surprisingly not by one of the police, but by the barman! He told me later, when the three had been led away in handcuffs, that if you tend bar in the East End, you soon learn how to deal with aggressive drunks! He said he'd only been working 'Up West' for a few months, and hadn't had much call on these skills recently. I gathered he was quite proud of himself – I treated him to a Scotch in gratitude!

The arresting officers at the pub said that the villains would be taken to West End Central Police Station, so that is where we shall go, once we've dealt with Mrs Abbott."

"DC Pratt is happy to go ahead and arrest her once we spot her, on the strength of what I witnessed her doing at the embassy," said Mel, "we shall have to be careful, of course – we can't afford to give her the chance to shoot anyone else!"

"Look," said Alex, "there are people emerging now – let's go, I've already settled up for our teas. Can you see Mrs Abbot, Mel?"

"Yes, she's the one in the brown coat and cloche hat. Let's cross over – I'll distract her and give Derek a chance to make an arrest."

Melpomene crossed the street, calling out, "Dorothy – wait for me!", and falling into step on Mrs Abbott's right, affectionately squeezing her arm.

"I'm dying to ask you about the shooting – I missed most of it! Did you see who did it – the police, I suppose?"

DC Derek Pratt overtook them and blocked their path, saying "I'm arresting you, Dorothy Abbot, for the use of a firearm to cause grievous harm!" and went into the routine cautionary address. She struggled to free her right hand, but Mel had a firm grip on her arm, and was able to prevent her drawing her little pistol, so that Alex could take it from her coat pocket as Derek was handcuffing her.

Less than an hour later, a group, including Alex and Mel, the officers involved in the arrests at the embassy and at the Five Bells, and DS Cec Thomson, bandaged up but smiling, and Jimmy Manley, was gathered in the main office of the CI department at West End Central, where Jimmy summarised all the events of the day and congratulated Mel and Alex on their parts in gathering in most of the active players in the conspiracy.

"In a few minutes," he said, "I'm expecting Deputy Commissioner Fitz-Hugh to arrive here and endorse my remarks, as well as making a special announcement concerning the Crabbe and Crabbe agency! Meanwhile, the canteen ladies are serving cakes, biscuits and tea – not, I should point out, in the station urn, but in a special teapot reserved for distinguished guests!"

Adrian Fitz-Hugh arrived and congratulated everyone, and then said, "I have a special message to read out from His Excellency, the Italian Ambassador. He would like me to convey his thanks to all members of the Metropolitan Police who have contributed to the success of this enterprise, and also to inform the principals and staff of the Crabbe and Crabbe agency that, as well as his congratulations and thanks, he has authorised the payment of a sum to them to cover their fees and out-of-pocket expenses. A cheque – drawn on a reputable bank – will be sent to the agency in the next few days. His Excellency spoke to me on these matters, and I can assure you, Mel and Alex, that he was deeply impressed."

Everyone in the room applauded at this!

"And now," went on Fitz-Hugh, "I would like to make a further announcement. Mr and Mrs Crabbe will have received in the post in the last day or two, an official Home Office statement endorsing their agency as a 'body ancillary to the Metropolitan Police Service'. I would like to stress that this award is by no means an empty and formal covenant, but that it has immediate practical implications. I will now announce the first of these – some of my colleagues in the Metropolitan Police, including DCI Manley, will already be aware of this – which concerns the formation, still in its early stages, of an international police collaboration service, between, so far, Denmark, the Netherlands, France – by way of the Sûreté Nationale – and similar bodies in Italy and Germany. As well as Crabbe and Crabbe being ancillary to the Met, this decision gives them a similar relationship to the international service, enabling them to call directly on its facilities, without going through my office as an intermediary."

He went on, "I said that this arrangement was by no means merely a formality, and to confirm this I now announce that, within the next day or two, Crabbe and Crabbe will receive a detailed proposal for their first case under these new conditions, which is to investigate a gang operating in London and environs, fortunately by no measure the English equivalent of the Mafia – the Crabbes have had skirmishes with its agents and branches more than once already. I should point out that they will still be free to pursue their own enquiries."

FIN

KEEP VIGILANT FOR THE NEXT CASE!

Crabbe and Crabbe's next case will be coming out soon!

Will there be murders? Who knows.

Will there be skullduggery? Undoubtedly.

Will Melpomene and Alex solve the case?

Of course – how could anyone doubt this!

Look out for:

"Up Against the Hoxton Mob"

A Case for Crabbe and Crabbe.

By Geoffrey Foster

Coming later this year.